# Gelignite

Born in Sydney, Australia, ~~~~~~~~~~~~~~~~
Australian National University, Canberra. He has ~~~~~~
journalist, proof-reader, teacher, mortuary attendant and process
worker, living in England, Belgium, Switzerland and Wales.

He has published three novels – apart from the *Yellowthread Street*
series – and has contributed to many magazines. He has also
written a number of radio and stage plays.

William Marshall now lives in Eire. His first two *Yellowthread*
novels – *Yellowthread Street* and *The Hatchet Man* – are also
published in Pan.

Previously published by
William Marshall in Pan Books

Yellowthread Street
The Hatchet Man

William Marshall
# Gelignite
A Yellowthread Street Mystery

**Pan Books** London and Sydney

First published in Great Britain 1976 by Hamish Hamilton Ltd
This edition published 1978 by Pan Books Ltd,
Cavaye Place, London SW10 9PG
© William L. Marshall 1976
ISBN 0 330 25296 8
Printed and bound in Great Britain by
Richard Clay (The Chaucer Press) Ltd, Bungay, Suffolk

for Ron and Val Fear

# Death by Water

Hop Pei Cove, on the western side of the Hong Kong police district of Hong Bay, smelled of fish. Not fresh, live fish, nor even dead fish, but fish long, long dead, not fresh, not yesterday's or the day before yesterday's fish, but extinct fish, obsolete fish, fish long gone to their fishy after-life, fish of a monumental and ancient age, antique fish, phantom fish, the ghosts of fish, fish drawn, quartered, gulleted, filleted, forked, fed into, finished and fishy. Fish of high, bygone and long dead odour. Stinking fish. Detective Inspector Phil Auden said, 'Blecht – fish!'

It was 5.30 in the morning on Fisherman's Beach at Hop Pei Cove and the driver of one of the police cars parked on the hard packed sand rubbed his hands together and opened a tin of rich smelling body wax to polish the decal on the door of the driver's side of his vehicle. The decal said HONG KONG POLICE on a banner below a picture of a nineteeth-century quayside scene surrounded by laurel leaves. He leaned forward into his task and saturated his fish-filled nostrils with the smell of the wax. A fisherman mending his nets and watching four detectives and two uniformed Constables in thigh-waders thigh-high in the water off the beach shook his head. He looked at the driver again and repaired a break in his net.

On the water, the wind changed and took the smell of fish back to the beach. Auden said, 'The wind's changed.' He drew a breath of relatively pure air. Something floated past him on the surface of the water and he reached for it with his rubber-gloved hands. It was a twig. He let it pass on the current.

Detective Senior Inspector Christopher Kwan O'Yee looked at him. O'Yee was a Eurasian, a little more used from his boyhood in San Francisco (another great stop on the International Fish Sniffer's World Route of Fish Sniffy Beaches), to odours of all ilks, but he still did not like sniffing fish. He glanced down at something near his section of the water. It was Auden's twig doing a quick circuit. He flipped it back to Auden. Auden looked at it and flipped it behind him towards the beach. The wind changed again.

Detective Chief Inspector Harry Feiffer asked, 'What was that?'

'A twig.'

'You're sure?'

Detective Inspector Spencer said, 'It was a twig.'

Doctor Macarthur's voice called out from somewhere near the resuscitation equipment in the ambulance near the waxed police car on the beach, 'What was that?' Resuscitation equipment meant nice deep whiffs of unfishy oxygen anytime you liked.

Macarthur called again, 'What was that?'

Feiffer called back, 'A twig!'

'A what?'

(Ambulances meant you didn't have to wade about waist high in dirty South China Sea effluvia and smell the smell of fish.)

'A bloody twig!'

'—Thank you!'

A little farther out in the effluvia Constable Sun called out, 'Here!' He touched at something an inch below the surface with his rubber glove. He called out again, 'Here!' and took a long plastic bag from a packet inside his shirt. He called out, 'It's a leg—' and opened the bag underwater to scoop it up.

Doctor Macarthur's head went zipp! – phew! out of the ambulance doors as he stuck his oxygen-filled Roman nose into the world to see what had happened. He called out, 'What's been found?'

'A leg!'

'Good! Good!'

Sun sealed the bag with a length of wire attached to it and went sloshing in towards shore dragging the leg and water-filled plastic bag a little behind him.

Spencer watched him go. Something else floated by and he leaned towards the surface of the water to see what it was. It was a fish. The fish swam off. 'What's the tally?'

O'Yee said, 'Part of a shoulder, two legs and a hand.'

Auden said, 'And part of a hip and pelvis.'

'Yeah.' O'Yee looked at the surface of the water for any further bits of the anatomical jigsaw. O'Yee said, 'The hip and pelvis were the bits found by the swimmer.'

Auden said, 'Anyone who swims in this muck at half-past four in the morning *deserves* to find a hip and pelvis.' He asked O'Yee, 'Did you take the call?'

'Constable Lee took it.'

Auden turned to Lee, a hundred feet away in the ragged line of waders, 'What was he doing at half-past four in the morning?'

'Who?'

'The person who reported finding the first part.'

Constable Lee said, 'He was swimming.' He looked across to where Constable Sun was dragging the plastic bag across the sand towards the ambulance and Doctor Macarthur was waiting like an anxious birthday-boy to receive it, 'He was out for a swim.'

'At half-past four in the morning?'

Lee watched as Sun handed the object to Macarthur and caught a heavy whiff of fish. Lee said, 'I don't think he'll be doing it again for a while.'

Feiffer ordered, 'Stop that talking. Keep spread out.' He was thinking of the work piling up at the Station and the faces of the North Point detectives who had agreed, grudgingly, to cover it. He said to Auden, 'I don't want anything missed.' He glanced at the beach and saw Sun wading back through the light swell as Macarthur carried his trophy into the ambulance, 'We need the complete body.' The wind changed again and he wished he had been born without his olfactory lobes. He said irritably to Spencer who was concentrating very hard on his particular part of the job, 'Just try and concentrate on your particular part of the job, will you?' and turned down windward.

A crowd had gathered along the beach sea-wall and stood like Roman spectators in an amphitheatre watching the disposal men dispose of the Christians after the lions had disposed of the Christians. Their muttering made a heavy humming sound and the wax-in-the-nose police driver thought briefly that he might go up and move them on, noted that the way to the wall was mined with the lethality of anti-personnel fishstinks, and decided against it. He glanced towards the open doors of the ambulance where the Government Medical Examiner was happily assembling parts of a body on a steel tray and took another blob of wax for the decal. He looked at the decal before blobbing it. The decal shone.

O'Yee shivered. Later, when the sun got higher, it would be a warm spring day, but now, up to his waist in night cold water, it was cold. He looked at the humming crowd and then back to the water. Something white was floating there, a few inches below the surface. He watched it come. It moved with the current and then turned in a little eddy below the surface. It was another hand. O'Yee closed his eyes and took out a plastic bag.

Spencer said, 'I've got something!' He said, 'Oh – Jesus—' He looked away.

O'Yee directed the mouth of the plastic bag over the hand and sealed the top.

Spencer said, 'It's a stomach—' His own turned. He took out a plastic bag with an effort of will and snared it.

Constable Lee said, 'I've got something!' It was a section of chest, still wearing a shirt. The shirt was waterlogged and torn. It seemed to be brown in colour. He took out his bag.

Auden looked at O'Yee and Spencer going towards the shore with their bags. Something touched him on the leg. He looked down expecting to see a fish. It was a head.

Feiffer said, 'What is it?'

Auden looked at him.

'Is it the head?'

Auden nodded.

Auden said, 'I can't guide it into the plastic bag—'

'Has it got any hair?'

Auden nodded. The head had strands of black hair floating out around it like seaweed.

Feiffer said, 'Pick it up by the hair.' He saw something next to his own leg and looked down to make out what it was. It was a section of shoulder. He took out a bag to get it.

The crowd on the wall went 'Oooo ...' Feiffer glanced across. Auden had the head by the hair and was trying to get it into the mouth of the bag. His hand slipped from the wet hair and the head fell back into the water with a splash. The crowd made a heavy moaning sound.

The section of shoulder floated neatly into the open plastic bag. Feiffer sealed the bag and held it below the water. He heard Auden say, 'Got it—!' and then the sound of him sloshing quickly in towards shore. Feiffer heard a heavy sigh from the crowd. He waited until O'Yee and Lee were back on station in the water and went in with the shoulder as Auden came sloshing back towards Spencer.

Spencer asked Auden, 'The head?'

Auden nodded.

Spencer asked, 'Young man or old?'

'Young.'

Spencer nodded. He said self-encouragingly, 'There isn't much more now.' He saw Feiffer reach the ambulance and hand his bag in to Macarthur through the open rear doors. Spencer looked at the crowd. They seemed very still. One of them seemed to ask the driver something, but the driver waved his hands to say he couldn't answer. The crowd seemed to make a heavy droning sound.

O'Yee said softly to someone, 'They're worried.'

He spoke very quietly and no one heard him.

O'Yee said, 'They're worried that we mightn't find all of him. Before we found the head it was just a pile of legs and arms and bits, but now we've found the head it's someone who's died in water.' He said, 'The Chinese have two great fears: drowning at sea and of being put into their graves with bits missing from them.' He said to Spencer, 'In the old days, the families of condemned men used to pay the axeman to sew the head back on the people he executed.' He said, 'It's a Chinese belief that the soul won't rest if the body's been lost at sea or dismembered.' He said to Spencer, 'I don't believe that.' He said in an odd voice, 'The European part of me says that it's a load of crap.' He looked down into the water and blinked at something.

Feiffer came back through the slight swell and took up his position. He asked Auden, 'Any more?'

'No. How much more to go?'

Feiffer looked back at the ambulance and the unseeable thing that was being assembled inside it on a steel tray. 'Not much.' He said hopefully, 'We'll be finished soon. It's a young man in his twenties, slightly undernourished, been in the water for six hours or so.' He said, 'Macarthur says that the lungs suggest he was dead when he went in.' He said quickly, 'So let's get it over with.' He shook his head to clear the picture of the inside of the ambulance.

A long way out in the cove a water police launch went by at top speed in the direction of Stanley Bay, its twin props slicing a foaming white cleavage of water away from its bow. There were two figures on the flying bridge and another in the stern. The launch changed course briefly for something, and then went around the point out of sight. Its trailing wake went from white to green and came to the shore as rolling eddies and waves. Spencer felt one of the little wavelets push against him and then travel past. He said to Feiffer, 'They'll never find anything—!'

'They're not looking. The current's bringing all the stuff in here. They're searching for wreckage.' He said defensively, 'They've been out since the first report this morning.' He looked at the wake coming towards him in progressively smaller undulations, 'Maybe they've found something already.'

O'Yee looked back at the crowd. They were still and silent. He thought, 'I'm not Chinese, I'm Eurasian, and the European side of me tells me it doesn't matter whether you drown, get shot, die of old age, or simply rust to pieces.' He thought, 'And it makes no difference whether you're found in one bit or thousands, you're just as dead.' He thought, 'The Chinese don't know what they're talking about.' He thought, 'Western science has just discovered after thousands of years that the Chinese knew what they were talking about with acupuncture.' He thought, 'And I read somewhere that the traditional Chinese cure-all, ginseng has just been found to really work.' He thought, 'The Chinese knew that all along.' He thought, 'But drowning, and souls, and being in bits, is just a load of crap.' The crowd on the sea-wall were totally silent. He thought, 'The European part of me knows it's a load of crap.' He thought, 'On balance, I prefer the Western side of my background.' Something floated past him, but it was only another twig. He thought, 'That's right.' He thought about the crowd. He said to himself, 'It's all nonsense.' He went to reach for the twig again and remembered it was the second time it had floated past. He flipped it firmly away with his hand and said to anyone or to no one, 'Twig.'

Feiffer rolled his rubber glove forward on to his knuckles to see his watch. It read 6 a.m. Water had seeped in through the glove and the watch and leather watchband were both wet. He wondered if it was waterproof. His wife had given it to him as a present. He thought, 'It must be. It says *Waterproof* on the back where she had my name engraved on it and she certainly wouldn't buy something that wasn't all it was supposed to be.' He thought, 'I wish I was at home.' He thought, 'I hope she hasn't heard about this on the radio.' He thought,

'Not now while she's pregnant.' He thought, 'I'd feel a bit funny about it if she knew I'd been touching dead things all morning.' He looked at the murky water, remembered the workload at the Station, and for no reason apparent to any of the others said, '*Shit—!*'

Spencer looked across at the beach. Doctor Macarthur had emerged from the ambulance and was motioning to them. He was shouting something, but Spencer couldn't make out the words. He looked quickly down at the water to check it was clear and then moved in closer to shore to hear what Macarthur was saying. A little way in towards the beach he saw something half submerged and went over to see what it was. It was a hand.

'Do you hear me?' Macarthur called out.

Spencer took out another plastic bag and moved it over the hand.

'The shoulders—' Macarthur called out, and then *something – something – something* – understand? It means—' and then, '*something – something – something—*'

Spencer closed the top of the plastic bag. He thought, 'A hand?' He thought, 'But we've—'

Macarthur called out, '—don't match – do you understand?'

'Oh my God!' Spencer said. They had already found two hands. He said, 'There are two of them!'

There was a hum from the crowd. Then talking and then someone – the crowd had grown and was a dark, solid mass along the stone wall of the beach front – shouted to someone close by, 'Gay-daw gaw yan?'

Feiffer nodded back to Macarthur and waved his hand. Macarthur acknowledged him and went hurriedly back inside the ambulance.

The voice in the crowd asked the driver on the beach insistently, 'Gay-daw?'

The driver shook his head.

Someone else in the crowd demanded, 'Leong gaw?' He was asking if it was true that there were two of them.

The driver nodded. He watched the six policemen in the water. There was a deep humming sound from the crowd, and then it fell silent.

O'Yee glanced at the crowd. They were like a dark cloth spread along the sea-wall with, here and there, specks and

13

flashes of colour from shirts and dresses, coats and bags. O'Yee thought, 'They're waiting to see if we find the other man.' He thought, 'The rest of the other man.' He thought, 'They're waiting to see if we understand about things and we're prepared to pay the executioner to sew the head back on.' He thought, 'They look like the drawings in old picture books of Chinamen standing on the rim of China looking out at the rest of the world.' He said to Feiffer, 'We are going to wait until we get it all, Harry, aren't we?'

'Yes.' Feiffer said, 'It's a murder job now. We have to get it all for identification.'

'Identification. Yes.'

O'Yee looked back to the crowd. He thought, 'My mother was Irish. She believed in all sorts of things.' He thought, 'My Chinese father doesn't believe in much at all.' He thought, 'He'd believe in this.' He glanced back at the crowd and felt their presence on him. He thought, 'They look like the drawings in old books.' He fixed his eyes on to the surface of the sea and looked for artifacts from antiquity.

Spencer straightened up. Then he leaned over and did something in the water.

Auden said, 'Well?'

'Nothing.'

Auden said, 'Don't get the idea you can go in the water if you want a piss. It pollutes the evidence.'

Spencer looked shocked. 'I was adjusting my waders!'

Feiffer said, 'Shut up and get on with it.' He felt in his shirt pocket with his wet gloves for his cigarettes, remembered he had left them in the car with his coat, and extracted his wet glove from his now equally wet pocket with distaste. Farther out, Constable Sun said, 'Sir—!' and bent down into the water to retrieve something. Feiffer went over. The water was colder and deeper and came up to his already saturated pocket and thoroughly flooded it. Sun had hold of something a little below the surface. He pulled it up and over like a waterlogged surfboard and pushed it in Feiffer's direction for his inspection. It was a complete body.

Constable Sun said quietly, 'Now there are three of them.'

Feiffer turned the body over. The face was pale and blotched, but at one time it had been a young male Chinese. There was a long ragged gash that ran from the left shoulder diagonally across the chest to the hip, and specks of white bone under the shirt showed where the flesh had been opened up to the ribs. It was a dull chopping wound made by a single sweep, but not deep enough to cause death unless by loss of blood. Feiffer said, 'You know what did it, don't you?' and Sun nodded. Feiffer said, 'I'll take the scruff of the neck and you guide the feet.'

They took the body in to the beach.

Spencer called, 'I've got another one! It's complete!' He called Auden over to help him take it in.

'Four.' O'Yee thought, 'There are four of them. We've got two complete ones and one Macarthur can put together, but we've only found a piece of the other one.' He heard someone in the crowd ask something and then someone else – probably the driver – shout an answer back and then there were the sounds of Feiffer and Sun and Auden and Spencer sloshing back into the sea from the beach.

Auden called out, 'Something else!' and O'Yee wondered how long it would be before the current changed and whatever else was out there in the sea floating into shore would be taken away for ever. He looked at the crowd, but it was silent and immobile.

Auden called out, 'An arm and part of a torso!' He called out to someone. 'It's the same! It's a ship's propeller wound! It isn't murder at all!' but O'Yee thought, 'That doesn't make any difference.' He looked at the crowd. They were beginning to edge forwards on to the beach and he thought, 'They *know*. They're keeping count and they *know*.' Macarthur's voice called, 'What was that?' and Spencer's voice called back, 'An arm! I've got an arm!'

O'Yee closed his eyes. He thought, 'My father was very particular about how and where his body was to be buried.' He thought, 'He showed me. He made it very clear to me what elder sons were supposed to do with their father's remains.' He looked at the crowd. The humming was there again. They were on the beach and the police driver was trying to get them to move back to the sea-wall. He thought, 'They won't move.' Something floated up against him and he looked down. It was a hand and an arm. He took out a plastic bag and guided them into the bag very carefully.

Feiffer looked over at him, but O'Yee took the bag and its

contents to shore without speaking. He passed the bag into Macarthur's charnel house in the back of the ambulance and went back into the sea.

The crowd watched him. The other three detectives were Europeans. There were two Chinese constables (three, if you counted the driver), but the four detectives were Inspectors and they were in charge. The crowd looked at him. They saw he was half-Chinese. He heard the humming.

The driver on the beach went quickly to the police car to answer the buzzing of the radio telephone. He motioned to O'Yee to wait, but O'Yee ignored him. The driver saw Feiffer watching him.

The driver nodded at something someone said on the radio – at a distance nodding into a telephone struck Feiffer as ludicrous (he wondered if he did it himself) – and then the driver came to the edge of the sand.

O'Yee said, 'It was an arm,' and Feiffer nodded.

Auden said, 'A leg and chest!' He bent down with his bag.

Feiffer asked O'Yee quietly, 'Are you all right, Christopher?'

'Yes.'

'They're propeller wounds. It looks like the four of them were caught up in a ship's propeller somewhere out at sea.' He said, 'Macarthur says they were already dead, so they must have drowned.' He looked down at the water, but there was nothing there.

Sun called, 'More!' He called to Feiffer, 'An arm!' He reached inside his shirt for his packet of plastic bags.

'Sir—' the driver's voice called out.

Feiffer shouted back, 'Yes?'

'The Water Police report they've stopped a junk full of illegal immigrants!' He called out again, 'Illegal immigrants! The Captain says four of them died and he threw the bodies overboard!'

At the water's edge Spencer said, 'Good old Water Police.'

Feiffer shouted back, 'How did they die?'

'What?'

'How did they *die*?'

'They suffocated! The Captain says it was an accident! The Water Police say you can leave it – they'll pick up whatever's left later! They say it isn't that important now!'

16

'OK!'

'They say leave it now—!'

'Right!'

'No!' O'Yee said.

Feiffer said, 'What was that?'

O'Yee said, 'There's still some missing.'

'What? Bodies?'

O'Yee looked down at the water. He heard the crowd humming. He thought, 'My father would have—' He said, *'Bits!'*

Spencer said suddenly, 'I've found the head!' His tone changed. He said, 'Oh ... God!' He leaned forward in the water to pick it up the way Auden had done.

Feiffer said, 'That's four.'

O'Yee said, 'There's still some missing.'

'What?'

'I don't know! I haven't been keeping bloody score!' He glanced back at the crowd. They *had* been keeping score and they knew there was still some missing. He said, 'Something! There's still some missing!' He shouted out to Macarthur at his ambulance, 'What's missing?'

'What?' Macarthur shouted back.

'Missing! What's still missing?'

Macarthur glanced back into his ambulance. 'A leg!' He shrugged. He shouted back, 'It's just a leg! Don't worry about it!' He shouted to them all as one. 'You can come in now!'

O'Yee said to Feiffer, 'There's a leg missing!'

'Does that matter?'

'Doesn't it?'

Feiffer looked across the cove. The current was changing with the beginning of the morning tide. He said, 'The tide's starting to turn. It'll be too late anyway in fifteen minutes.' He said, 'We've done pretty well, considering, and if the Water Police are certain it isn't a murder investigation—'

'It's because they're bloody Chinese, isn't it!'

'What the hell are you talking about?'

'If they were bloody Europeans you'd think it mattered!'

Feiffer said, 'I'm not even going to answer that one.' He said with concern in his voice, 'I don't know what's gotten into you, Christopher. I know this has been a bloody awful job, but you've seen worse—'

17

Macarthur called out, 'You can leave it now! I'm taking the ambulance in!' He went to the cab of the ambulance and roused the driver to shut the back doors.

O'Yee said, 'I just think we should find all of it, that's all.'

'There isn't the time. We could be here for the rest of the week.' He called to Auden and Spencer, 'OK, you can go in now—!' Feiffer looked over to Sun and Lee. 'You can go now. Off you go.'

Sun and Lee hesitated. They looked at O'Yee.

'Go on,' Feiffer said.

Sun and Lee looked at the crowd.

Feiffer said, 'That's an order!'

Sun said, 'Yes, sir.' He glanced at Lee and made a motion of resignation with his head. He and Lee waded past with Auden and Spencer.

Feiffer said to O'Yee, 'And you too.'

On the beach the ambulance passed through the crowd and out of sight.

O'Yee said, 'I think we should stay and find the leg.'

'No.'

'I think we should.'

'Why?'

'I – I just think we should, that's all.'

'The Water Police'll find it, or it'll be washed up on the evening tide, or tomorrow. Maybe never. It's just a leg. If it was a head it'd be different, but after all, it's only a bloody leg—'

'I think we should stay.'

Feiffer looked at him. He said, 'Unless you can give me some sort of strong reason, you can forget it. For all I know you just have a fascination about putting all the little wooden pieces together in bloody puzzles and jigsaws. For all I know, you—'

'You shut your goddamned mouth!'

'What the *hell* is the matter with you?'

'Nothing's the matter with—'

Feiffer said evenly, 'I'm ordering you to go to shore and that's all there is to it. We'll probably hear the leg's been found tomorrow or the next day and that'll all be fine and neat, but we do have other cases current in this district and I'm not about to waste all my detectives for the rest of the

18

bloody day just to find a bit of dead meat that's probably been eaten by the bloody fishes anyway! *Now bloodywell get back to shore!*

O'Yee looked at the beach. The crowd were moving forward past Auden and Spencer to where Sun and Lee took off their waders by the second police car. Sun said something to Lee and they both got quickly into the vehicle and drove off. The crowd turned to the shoreline and looked out at O'Yee.

Feiffer said, 'Go on. In.'

'I'd like to stay, Harry.'

'No.'

'I mean it.'

'So do I. We've got other work and it's just as important – more so.'

'If you could just spare me for—'

'No.'

O'Yee said, 'You can't have any objection if I—' He said, 'This isn't the scene of a possible crime anymore. I mean, now anyone can come here and—'

'Anyone who's off duty. But you're not.'

O'Yee looked at the crowd. He said, 'I meant, *them*!'

'They can do what they like.'

O'Yee said, 'I've never had very much time for religion or – for that sort of thing ...'

Feiffer began wading in towards the shore.

O'Yee thought, 'If I call out to them – to the crowd – they'll come in and look for the leg because they all believe it.' He thought, 'They ought to. Maybe they don't.' He thought, 'Maybe it's just me. Maybe it's the European side of me trying to be so goddamned Chinese there isn't a Chinese on earth who'd know what the hell I was talking about.' He thought, 'Maybe I'm imagining it all. Maybe they're just curious ghouls counting the grisly remains.' He thought, 'If I don't call them, I'll imagine they'll all be looking at me and feeling disgusted.' He thought, 'And if I do call them and they don't know what I mean, I'll look foolish.' He thought, 'It'll be a loss of face, Chinese or no.' He thought, 'They're all from this district: I have to make them take me seriously as a policeman or I'll be finished.' Something in the water bumped against his knee. He thought, 'If I don't say anything I'll never know.'

Feiffer said irritably, thinking of the caseload, 'Are you coming?'

The object bumped his knee again. 'O'Yee thought, 'I'll never know.' He knew what the object was without looking at it. He took out a plastic bag and bent down to recover it.

He took the leg into shore with a puzzled expression on his face.

# 1

As usual they were tearing Yellowthread Street down preparatory to rebuilding it up. Or, they were rebuilding it up preparatory to tearing it down. It was a mess. It was a mess five times a year. Five times a year Yellowthread Street was torn down or rebuilt. Standing outside his ivory shop on the corner of Canton Street, Mr Leung sighed. A giant pneumatic hammer went hammer, hammer, hammer, hammer, HAMMER! in the foundations of a torn-down or rebuilt office block; there was someone working with a nail gun high up on the flat roof of a half demolished post office branch (soon to be a bank office branch): POW! POW! POW! POW-POW! (as someone else with a nail gun gunned nails); a climbing crane balancing a half ton block of cement for the third floor of someone's prestigious development went grind, grind-snort! as it turned on its unoiled axis, and the traffic: the traffic, as usual, went roar! honk! roar! skreech! towards the new flyover near Beach Road.

Mr Leung, a sedate, prosperous man in his middle fifties who sometimes regretted his decision to enter commerce and not a monastery, sighed.

In the Detectives' Room of the Yellowthread Street Police Station, Auden shouted at the top of his voice, 'I'M GOING DEAF!'

Someone out in the corridor – one of the uniformed men – shouted back, *'Shut up!'*

Auden shrieked, *'I'm going bloody deaf!'*

The noise went HAMMER! HAMMER! HAMMER! POW! HAMMER! POW! POW! ROAR! HAMMER! HAMMER! SKREECH! HONK! HONK! POW! and then there was a pause and then it all went HAMMERPOWHONK

ROARHAMMERHAMMERPOWPOWPOWROARHAM-
MER – *HAMMER* ! ! ! !

Mr Leung considered the eternal philosophic dilemma of the noise frightening customers away from his store or the noise driving customers into his store, and considered in evidential reflection, his receipts.

Auden screamed, 'Deaf! It's sending me deaf! I'm going deaf I tell you! *Deaf!!*'

Five times a year. Autumn, Spring, Summer and Winter and whenever someone lost his fortune and sold off his Hong Bay real estate for redevelopment or someone else made his fortune and bought it.

Auden ripped open the street window and yelled out into the street. 'Shut – *up!*'

Feiffer shouted, 'Shut that window!'

Someone passing in the street looked up at Auden and shouted up, *'What?'*

Feiffer shouted, 'SHUT THE WINDOW!'

The someone in the street shouted up to Auden, 'I *can't hear you!*'

Auden shut the window.

ROARHAMMERPOWHAMMERHONKSKREECH-
ROARPOWPOWHAMMERHONK – HAMMER! POW! *HAMMER!*

Spring in Hong Bay.

The passing someone in the street, for no apparent reason, to no apparent person, yelled at the top of his lungs, *'SHUT – UP!!!!'*

8 a.m.

R-O-A-R! ... HAMMER! ! ! !

Sigh ...

Nicola Feiffer waddled across the living room of her third floor apartment on her bare feet and felt sludgy. She thought, 'Sludgy, that's how I feel.' She looked down at the pregnant sludge of her body and thought she was pure sludge from one end to the other. She looked at the brass carriage clock on the mantelpiece and wondered how metal managed to stay so slim and constant and unbulging. She thought, 'Sludge.' She waddled across to the divan, deposited her sludge into the upholstery and felt—

—sludgy.

She looked at the newspaper television programme. Nothing started for hours. She thought, 'I can't even be bothered to get out of my dressing gown.' She thought, 'And I'm certainly not going to try to make myself look presentable.' She thought, 'I hate everyone.' She thought, 'Everyone.' She leaned over and picked up the phone to ring her husband.

Her husband shouted, *'WHAT?'*

She hung up.

The noise stopped. There seemed to be no good reason why it did, but it stopped.

The postman took a handkerchief away from his nose, coughed a lungful of unoiled crane, pneumatic hammer, nail gun and traffic dust out from his bronchial tubes and said to Mr Leung outside his shop, 'It's stopped.' He handed Mr Leung a packet of letters held together with a rubber band. He said hopelessly to Mr Leung, 'They're probably all bills.'

'Hmm,' Mr Leung said. He took the packet of letters without looking at them.

'Or cheques,' the postman said.

'Hmm,' Mr Leung said. He glanced upwards at a maze of bamboo scaffolding on the soon-to-be (or once-had-been) prestigious office block development across the road.

The postman said, 'Maybe a rich relative in America's died and left you his oil wells in Texas.'

'Hmm,' Mr Leung said. He sighed and thought of the peace and tranquillity of the monastic life where a man of mature spirit might come to grips with the great questions of life and the cosmos.

The postman said, 'Or Arabia, that's the place to have an oil well these days.' He said, 'There's an Arab on my beat, but he's a clerk or something for El Al.' He said on reflection, 'That's a Jewish airline, isn't it? Maybe he isn't an Arab after all.' He said, 'He's got an Arab name.' He said to himself, 'How should I know?' He said consolingly to Mr Leung, 'Maybe one of the letters is good news.' He asked Mr Leung hopefully, 'What do you think?'

'Hmm,' Mr Leung said. He turned to go back inside his shop.

The postman said, 'You never know, do you?' He knew there was a letter in his bag to one of the detectives at the

Police Station written in the same hand as one of the letters for Mr Leung. He said happily to Mr Leung, 'I hope everything's all right.'

'Hmm,' Mr Leung said. He did not turn around. He put the letters on his little oak desk by the wall and went to check the price tags on his new stock and thought if there was one thing that always brought his monastic contemplation back to reality with a nasty bump in the mornings it was a chatty postman.

He said to himself, 'Hmmm.'

He sniffed.

O'Yee said, 'They're probably on strike.' At times like these it was one of the great consolations of the cruel capitalist system, 'They're probably knocking off for half an hour to complain.' He said to Auden, 'They'll probably work an extra two hours this evening to make up for it.' He asked Feiffer, 'Who was that on the phone?'

Feiffer looked up from a pile of forms, 'What was that?' He wriggled his finger in his ear to make sure that the silence wasn't an auditory hallucination.

O'Yee asked, 'Who was that on the phone?'

'Just then?'

'Yes.'

'I don't know. They rang off as soon as I answered.' He said without feelings about it one way or the other, 'Probably just another nut.' He went back to his forms and corrected a spelling mistake with his fountain-pen.

Auden said, 'Have any of you seen that crane they've got out on that new building opposite Canton Street?' He went to the closed window and opened it exploratorily. The noise did not start again. He said, 'It's carrying around the biggest blocks of cement I've ever seen in my life.' He poked his head out of the window to catch sight of the climbing crane anchored to the top of the half built block. He said, 'If they ever let go of one of those loads you'd hear the crash half way to Peking.' He said to Spencer, 'When I was a kid I used to like watching cranes.'

'Really?' Spencer asked. He said, 'Where was—' His phone rang. He picked it up and said, 'Spencer ... oh.' He glanced furtively around the room, bent forward at his desk and cupped his hand around the mouthpiece. He said very softly, 'Hullo, Frank ...'

Auden said to O'Yee, 'When I was a kid, I used to like watching the cranes move when the chasers signalled them. They used to blow a whistle or make signals with their hands.'

O'Yee looked interested, 'What are they called again?'

'Crane chasers.'

O'Yee said, 'I've never heard that one before.' He asked, 'What exactly is a—' His phone rang. He picked it up and said, 'O'Yee ... yes.' He paused. He said, 'Oh. Oh, well ... yes, sir ...' His eyes flicked cautiously around the room. He bent forward a little at his desk and cupped his hand around the mouthpiece. He said, 'Oh ... yes, sir ... Oh.'

Auden said to Feiffer, 'A crane chaser is the man who gives the signals to the crane driver from the ground.'

Feiffer looked up from his forms and then at the open window. He asked Auden irritably, 'Who opened that window?'

'I did.' Auden said, 'He's the man who gives the signals from the ground.'

'Who is?'

'The crane chaser.'

'What crane chaser?'

Auden said, 'Any crane chaser!' He looked at Spencer, but Spencer was smiling amiably into the telephone and saying 'Yes ... hmmm ... yes, Frank ...' and O'Yee, looking more serious, was nodding at his phone and saying very efficiently, 'Hmm ... yes ... hmmm,' and scribbling something down in his personal notebook. Auden said, 'I used to watch them when I was a kid.'

Feiffer's forms were well and truly fouled up. 'Who?'

'Crane chasers! !' Auden said hopelessly, 'Ah, forget it!'

Feiffer said, 'And close that bloody window, will you?'

The postman came up the stairs of the Yellowthread Street Police Station. He nodded to Ah Pin, the aged cleaner near the front desk, and then to Constable Sun behind the desk. He said to Pin, who had never had a letter in his life, 'Nothing today,' and Ah Pin smiled and went on sweeping dust with his broom. The postman said, to Constable Sun, 'How are things with the law?'

'Not so bad. How's everything with you?'

The postman paused. He wiped his brow. He deposited his packet of letters held together with a rubber band on to Sun's desk. He wiped his brow again. '*Ngai sai gai* – slaving through the world.' He sighed.

'Hmm,' Constable Sun said. That seemed to be the end of that conversation. He said pleasantly to the postman, 'See you tomorrow.' He waited for the postman to go.

The postman didn't.

Constable Sun glanced at the postman. The postman watched Constable Sun.

Constable Sun said, 'Is there anything else?'

'Hmm,' the postman said. He winked at the letters on Constable Sun's desk. He said, 'Hmm-hmmm. Hmm.'

The postman left.

In his ivory shop, a hundred and fifty yards from the Police Station, Mr Leung sat at his desk to open his mail. There were six letters in all. He glanced at the envelopes: one was definitely a circular from the Hong Bay Chamber of Commerce (he put that to one side, by a nineteenth-century glass inkwell filled with black ink), three more were bills from his suppliers (he sighed and opened them with a silver paper-knife and spiked them on the cast iron spike by his elbow), one was a statement from his bank, and the last was a long manilla envelope that felt slightly heavy, addressed in a hand that he did not recognize.

He thought he would open that after he had read the bad news from the bank. He put it to one side with the Chamber of Commerce envelope and slit open the bank letter.

Spencer said very softly into the phone, 'Yes ... goodbye ... yes.' He listened for a moment, 'Goodbye, Frank ... yes.' He smiled. 'Yes, goodbye.' He hung up.

Auden said, 'Who was that?'

'Frank.'

'Frank who?'

'No one.' Spencer said absently to Auden, 'What was that you were talking about, Phil? Crane drivers?'

'Crane *chasers*—'

'Oh, yes ...'

Feiffer asked Spencer, 'Who was that on the phone?' His own phone rang and he said, 'Feiffer.'

Spencer said quietly, 'Frank.'

Auden said, 'I used to watch them, you know, when I was a kid. They used to be on the docks – that was where you saw them mainly, working with the cranes that unloaded the—'

O'Yee hung up his phone. He said, 'Ah-hah!' He said again, 'Ah-HAH!' He called over to Feiffer with an odd gleam in his eye, 'I'm going out for a while, OK?'

Feiffer said to his wife, 'Hang on a second.'

'I'm going out for a while, all right?'

'Who was that?'

'Who?'

'On the phone.' Feiffer said to Spencer, 'And you, who were you talking to?'

'Frank,' Spencer said.

O'Yee said, 'Kan.'

Spencer said, 'It was personal.'

O'Yee said, 'Confidential.'

Auden looked at Feiffer. Feiffer said to his wife at the other end of the line, 'Hang on a second.'

Auden said to Spencer, '—unloaded the ships. They used to—'

O'Yee said, 'I'm going out. OK? I'll be back soon.'

Spencer said, 'I wouldn't mind a break myself a little later—'

Feiffer said, 'What do you mean: "personal", "confidential"?'

Auden said, '—you'd see them—'

'It was a personal matter.'

O'Yee said, 'Confidential.'

Feiffer said to his wife— He said to O'Yee, 'Go on then.' His wife said at her end of the line, 'So I was thinking I might get a pet of some sort to keep me company for the next few weeks – until it's due.' She said, 'I thought perhaps a cat.'

'It's against the terms of the lease.'

'Is it.'

'Yes.'

'What about a dog?'

'The same.' Feiffer said to Auden, 'Haven't you got anything to do?'

Auden said to Spencer, 'Crane chasers—' Spencer's phone rang. Spencer said without asking who it was, 'Frank—' and smiled and settled back to enjoy the call.

'How about a rabbit or something?'

'A what?' Feiffer asked Auden, 'Well?'

'Well, how about a tortoise?'

'You can't housetrain a tortoise.' He said to Auden, 'Go and collect the mail or something. Don't just stand around doing nothing.' Feiffer said to his wife, 'They stink. And they hibernate in winter and get insects.'

Nicola Feiffer said, 'I'd like something.'

'Why?'

There was a silence at the end of the line. Nicola Feiffer glanced at the slim carriage clock. She glanced at the television programme that said television programmes didn't start for ages. She glanced at the four walls. She looked at her sludge. She counted the hours in two more weeks of pregnancy. She— She shouted down the line, 'What do you mean, "why?"!'

Mr Leung put his bank statement to one side and took up his old-fashioned nib pen. He made a series of cautious calculations and sighed. He shook his head. There was a briar pipe in a little ivory pipe holder and he took it up and considered its empty bowl.

He put it in his mouth, took it out again, considered the bank statement and the calculations from another angle, moved his nib pen to the centre of his desk, put down his pipe again and took up the last envelope to slit it open.

It seemed a little stiff and he had trouble starting the flap with the point of his knife.

Feiffer began opening the single letter Auden brought in from the front desk with one hand. It was addressed to Feiffer care of the Detectives' Room and bore a Hong Bay postmark. He said sympathetically to Nicola, 'I know how you feel of course—'

'You damn well *don't* know how I feel!'

He got his little finger under the flap and ripped open the letter.

Nicola Feiffer demanded at the other end of the line, 'Well, do you? How could you?'

Mr Leung's paper-knife slipped on the glue-dried flap and nicked him on the finger. That was all this particular Monday morning needed. He put the letter to one side and ripped open one of the circulars. It was for something he didn't need. He ripped open the second. It was a duplicate of the first. He threw the third into a wastepaper basket unopened.

He went back to the first envelope and tried the paper-knife on it for the second time.

The letter to Feiffer said:
*Leung. Political.*
There was no signature.

There seemed to be some sort of very thin wire sticking out from the seam join of the envelope. It protruded about an eighth of an inch. Mr Leung glanced at it and wondered what it was connected to.

Mr Leung opened the letter.

Feiffer said irritably to the single sheet of notepaper, 'Another bloody nut—!'

The explosion tore everything apart. Mr Leung had the sensation of something lifting him upwards and back on a giant gust of red hot air, like a typhoon, and then there was a stinging sensation in his stomach and a chaos of papers being blown around the room. The papers went on blowing around the room for a long time, then they fell back to the earth and were still.

Mr Leung felt that he was watching the room from somewhere higher. It was strange. He saw the papers lying on the floor, charred, some of them burning, and his desk overturned and shattered as if someone had hit it with a mallet and he thought, 'It must have been one of those pneumatic hammers.' He saw two objects covered in cloth lying by the desk, one on top of the other and he thought, 'I don't know what they are. They weren't in my shop.' There was something soft, like mud, oozing down his pelvis. He looked down to see what it was.

He saw what it was and then looked back to the two cloth-covered objects by the desk. He realized what they were and looked back to his chest. The spike was embedded in his chest, pinning him to the rear wall. There seemed to be a gap somewhere on the wall between his pelvis and the floor.

The black stuff seemed to go on oozing and oozing. He knew the two objects by the desk were his legs. He thought, 'I'm taking this much too calmly.' He thought, 'This can't be real.'

It was. He thought, 'I wonder what's going to happen to-morrow.' He thought, 'I don't know what it is I'm waiting for to come to an end, but it seems to be going on for such a long time.' He felt a little sad. He thought, 'I wonder why that is.' He thought, 'There's an odd smell in here.' He thought, 'It must be the explosive.' He thought—

His body stopped oozing its life and he died.

Auden said, 'They've dropped the load on the crane!' Dust still continued to fall down from the ceiling of the Detectives' Room. He wrenched open a window and looked out at the crane. The load was intact.

Spencer said, 'What the hell was it?'

All the phones in the Station began ringing simultaneously.

# 2

As the crowd began to gather outside what was left of Mr Leung's ivory shop in Yellowthread Street, Detective Senior Inspector Christopher Kwan O'Yee was savouring the delights of the good life two miles away at the Hong Bay Millionaires' Club. O'Yee was enjoying it. He sat back in his heavy black lacquered carved wooden chair and said to Conway Kan, one of the selfsame millionaires, 'Thank you very much.'

Conway Kan sat back in his heavy black lacquered chair (the carving just a little richer and the lacquer just a little heavier) and nodded. He was a very urbane fellow. He said urbanely, 'I'm just delighted you could make the time to see me.' He nodded in the direction of a series of paintings on the wall depicting the Imperial Court during the Fifty Thousand Hong Kong Dollars A Picture Dynasty and said, 'The pictures are always worth a visit even if the members of the Club aren't.'

O'Yee smiled. He thought, 'I'll bring my kids and have them eat ice cream on the antiques.' He said, 'I've never been here before.'

'No?' Conway Kan looked surprised. He was a very urbane fellow. He made a surprised motion with his head, 'I suppose the members aren't really very social.' He said, 'As one gets older one appreciates solitude.' He looked like the eternal Chinese, anywhere between fifty and seventy years old, portly, prosperous and balding, a pleasant-faced version of Mao Tse Tung without the warts. He touched absently at the lapel of his English lightweight suit and said, 'Is your family well? Your wife, Emily, and your children, Patrick, Penelope and Mary?' Conway Kan added, 'Shall I have tea brought?'

O'Yee shook his head. 'How did you—'

Conway Kan smiled. It was the sort of smile that meant you were either going to get a tip on the stockmarket that would make you a multi-millionaire overnight or the sort of smile that meant you had disappointed someone and consequently you might as well go out and slit your wrists because, oh boy, no one in the civilized world was ever going to have anything to do with you ever again because the word was out. Conway Kan said, 'Mr Ho was kind enough to advise me that you were a man one could discuss things with. Naturally, I inquired about your family.'

'Mr Ho?'

'I believe his first name is Humphrey. Is he in – Special Branch?'

'So I hear.' Ho was one of those famous Hong Bay characters one heard about but never actually met. O'Yee said, 'I've never actually met him.'

'He knows your senior officer, Mr Feiffer, and, of course, Mr Feiffer knows you.' Conway Kan flicked an invisible speck (gold dust) from the bridge of his nose, 'One proceeds discreetly when seeking men of discretion.'

O'Yee said, 'I have no intention of doing anything illegal.' He waited for Conway Kan to be offended.

Conway Kan was not offended. He smiled again. 'Precisely why you were recommended to me.' He said, 'Being a Eurasian has its advantages. For you.'

O'Yee waited.

'You combine the patience of your Chinese father with the efficiency of the Western influences in your life.' Conway Kan said, 'Your father is very highly respected in the community.'

'My father lives in San Francisco.'

Conway Kan said, 'So do many of my friends and business acquaintances.' He said again, 'Your father is considered a man of merit.' He looked, briefly, like an octopus spreading its tentacles from one side of the known world to the other. He said, 'You will have to accept my word that my, um' – he paused – 'my small success in the material world was gained honestly.' He asked, 'Do you accept that?'

Tentatively, O'Yee nodded. He thought, 'I've heard about this man. All he has to say is "Hmm," and you spend the rest of your life with the same credit rating as the Rockefellers and two Swiss banks combined.' He said, 'You're relatively speaking, a very anonymous man.'

Conway Kan smiled again. That pleased him. One did not advertise wealth, especially when the spring kidnapping season was on. He said, 'One tries neither to advertise good works nor wealth.' He added quickly, 'If one possesses it.'

O'Yee thought, 'Wealth or good works?' He thought, 'What am I getting into?'

Conway Kan said, 'I am unmarried, Mr O'Yee.' (Briefly, O'Yee looked worried.) He said, 'The family affection I hold is for my parents who are, sadly, no longer in person on this earth.' He said, 'As well as treasuring their memory I have an irrational affection for certain material objects that, to me, have their associations attached to them.' He went on quickly in case his meaning was not crystal clear, 'My father was a poor man. I refer therefore to objects which may appear to be of little monetary worth.' He glanced at the pictures on the wall representing the days of a fixed Empire and China's place at the centre of the world, 'It is, of course, very important to me that I appear to be completely in control of my faculties.' He asked pleasantly, 'You take my drift, of course?'

O'Yee nodded. There was nothing worse for business than a millionaire without all his marbles. He asked, 'How can I help you?' He thought, 'This is getting a little too Chinese for me.' He said, 'Sometimes I don't feel very Chinese.'

Conway Kan looked at him.

'I don't know why I said that.'

Conway Kan said, 'I do.' O'Yee wanted to ask him whether it was true about dismembered bodies and crowds and mythologies. Conway Kan said, 'It is how other people think of you that is important.' He glanced at the series of pictures on the wall, 'There is a sale of pictures quite soon in the Connaught Room of the Mandarin Hotel.' He asked, 'Were you aware of the sale?'

'I read about it somewhere.'

'Do you intend to bid on any of the pictures?'

O'Yee thought, 'You must be joking!' He said, 'No.'

Conway Kan said urbanely, 'Lot number twenty-six will be extremely reasonable in price. It is generally thought to be a later copy of a work by a famous eighteenth-century artist.' He said, 'My experts tell me that it is, on the contrary, genuine.' He said, 'A thrifty man would be well advised to invest in such a work.' He said, 'I mention it in passing because I, alas, will be indisposed by illness at the time of the sale and will not therefore be able to bid on the work.' He said, 'I believe the sale will be held some time in the next three or four weeks.'

O'Yee paused. He tried being Chinese. 'I'm sorry to hear about your future illness.'

It worked. Conway Kan said, 'I appreciate your solicitude.'

O'Yee said, 'I'm glad we met. It is a good thing for a police officer to be well acquainted with the people his duty it is to assist.' He said, 'Small matters he might be in a position to deal with might otherwise not come to his attention.' He said, 'The concerns of the law-abiding are as much his task as the calumnies of criminals.' He thought, 'That was a good one.' He thought, 'I wish I had the nerve to try a few proverbs.'

Conway Kan said, 'Men are good or bad according to their conduct; and their misery or happiness depends on themselves.' He repeated in Mandarin, *'Shan o sui jen tso 'huo fu tzu chi chao.'* He smiled.

O'Yee said, 'Good men get cheated; as good horses get ridden.' He changed from Cantonese to Mandarin and said, *'Jen chung yu chih shu, shih shang wu –* um—'

*'—chih jen,'* Conway said helpfully.

*'Chih jen.'*

Conway Kan said, 'Quite true.' He said, 'I am very glad we met.' He said, 'May I ask you, dear friend—' (O'Yee thought, 'I'm going to be rich! I'm going to be filthy rich!') '—to assist me in a small matter?'

'Ask.'

Conway Kan said, 'I have lost something.' He said, 'It is

32

a thing of small value to anyone but myself and it is a matter I should like to keep between men of discretion like ourselves—' (O'Yee thought, 'Rolling in it! Lighting cigars with thousand dollar notes! Mysterious phone calls in the night saying "Buy Hong Kong Codpieces Limited" – millions on the Stock Exchange!') Conway Kan said, 'It is an object that belonged to my father and has been lost.'

O'Yee asked, 'Stolen?'

Conway Kan opened his hands.

'I see.'

Conway Kan said sadly, 'It is not a matter for jocularity.' He glanced skywards to show that the world was full of men who, unlike themselves, had no respect for The Way. He said, 'It is a Ramphastes Toco in a state of perfect antique preservation.'

O'Yee paused.

'It has been lost.' Conway Kan said, 'To make this fact known would give rise to certain attempts at crude humour that men like ourselves would find distressing and base.'

O'Yee nodded. He thought, 'What the hell is a Ramphastes Toco?'

Conway Kan leaned forward a little in his seat. He dropped his voice. He said conspiratorially, 'You are aware what a—'

'I'm afraid I—'

Conway Kan lowered his voice even lower. He smiled one of his smiles. He said, 'Ah, my dear friend—'

O'Yee waited. He tried to look inscrutable.

Conway Kan said, 'Dear friend, I have lost my stuffed toucan.' He said quickly to explain all the machinations for evil and loss of face and malicious double-dealing in the world, 'You see? "Conway Kan's toucan." "I can, Conway Kan too," "Toucan if one can—"' He said sadly, 'You see?' He asked, 'Are such things amusing? Do you find such things humorous?'

O'Yee's face started moving of its own accord. He gritted his teeth.

'Well?' Conway Kan asked. He suddenly seemed like a very small old man.

'No.'

Conway Kan nodded. He said pleasantly, 'You will allow me the honour of inviting you to refreshments in the Members' Rooms?' He stood up to show O'Yee the way.

'Thank you.' O'Yee stood up. He had never heard of the Members' Rooms. No one had. He followed Conway Kan through a lacquered door.

Conway Kan said, 'There are some interesting antiques for the enjoyment of Members that you may find interesting to examine.' He stood aside and let O'Yee enter first. He said, 'I appreciate your sparing the time.'

O'Yee nodded. He felt more Chinese than Confucius.

They went into the Hong Kong holy of holies to discuss, as equals, one of life's little vicissitudes.

Spencer's phone rang. It was Nicola Feiffer. She asked pleasantly, 'Is Harry there, Bill?'

'No, I'm sorry, he's out.' Spencer said, 'There's a job on. I don't know when he'll be back.' He offered, 'I can probably get in touch with him if you like.'

'No. It isn't important.' (Spencer thought he heard her change positions in a chair with an effort.) 'I just wanted to talk to him, that's all. It doesn't matter if he's too busy.'

Spencer said quickly, 'It isn't that. He really has got a job on.' He said earnestly, 'He'd never pretend to be out when you rang. I've seen him almost leap at the phone when you call.' He waited.

There was a pause. Spencer said, 'Honestly.'

'Hmm.'

'Really – honest.' He asked, 'Are you still there?'

Nicola said, 'You haven't had too much experience catering to the neurotic whims of pregnant females, have you?'

There was a silence. Nicola said, 'Bill?'

Spencer said, 'I don't know what to say.' He glanced hopefully at the door of the Detectives' Room, but anybody who had had experience with the neurotic whims of pregnant females was distinctly reticent about using the door to come in. He said, 'I don't think you're neurotic.'

There was a long neurotic pause.

Nicola said, 'How are you getting along? It must be a change from Police Administration.' She asked, 'How long is it now you've been a detective?'

'Eighteen months.' Spencer said, 'Did you hear Christopher O'Yee got his promotion to Senior Inspector?'

'Yes.'

Spencer said, 'He deserves it, don't you think?'

There was another pause. Spencer tried to think of something to say. He wondered what she was doing at the other end of the line. He thought, 'It must be lonely for her by herself.' He said, 'Um—'

There was a sudden sound. It sounded like she sniffed, cleared her throat, and then sniffed again. Nicola said, 'Harry tells me you keep getting mysterious phone calls from someone named Frank.' She said, 'Is there any chance that Frank is short for Frances, with an *e*?'

'Frankie.' Spencer glanced at the door to check that no one was there. He lowered his voice. He said, 'Yes.'

'A girl?'

'Well – yes.'

'Personal?'

Spencer cleared his throat. 'Yes.'

Nicola Feiffer said, 'I'm delighted.' She said, 'I always thought you were the nicest one of the lot down there.' She said, 'It's about time you met a girl who appreciated you.' Nicola asked, 'She does appreciate you, doesn't she?'

Spencer thought of Frank. He said, 'Well, um—'

'Is she pretty?'

Spencer said, 'Beautiful!' He went red. He said quickly, 'Well, I mean—' He said, 'Well, I think so – um—' He asked to change the subject, 'It can't be too long now before the baby's due. Is it two weeks or three?'

Nicola Feiffer made a disgusted, due in two weeks or was it three noise in the back of her throat, 'Who cares?' There was another of those frightening pauses. 'Who bloodywell cares?'

Spencer wished that someone would come through the door. He had a brainwave, 'Well, Harry does anyway.' He said, 'He talks about nothing else. He seems absolutely delighted about it.'

There was just another pause. Spencer thought, 'Now I've done it!'

Nicola Feiffer said, 'Does he? Is Harry pleased?'

'Yes, of course.'

'Really?'

'Yes,' Spencer said, 'of course he is. Wouldn't anybody be?'

'Is *he*?'

'Of course.'

Nicola Feiffer said irritably, 'You keep saying "of course" as if it should be part of the human condition to be pleased. Maybe it is. But is *he*?'

'Hasn't he said so?'

'Has he said so to *you*?'

Spencer was about to say, 'Of course.' He thought that mightn't be such a good idea. He said, 'He's said so to everyone.'

'How would you know?'

'What?'

'How would you know about everyone? I don't think he's said so to anyone. He obviously hasn't said so to you.' She demanded miserably, 'Has he?'

'Of course he has!' He said, 'He's pleased!'

'Would you tell me if he wasn't?'

'No!' He said quickly, 'Yes!' He said, on a third thought, 'He's pleased.'

There was a long silence.

He said, 'Nicola, are you there? Is that all right?'

There was another pause. Then it ended. Nicola Feiffer said, 'Do you know what I dislike most about you?'

There was nothing to say to that.

Nicola Feiffer said, 'Your trouble, Spencer, is that you're just too bloody *nice*!' She hung up ferociously.

Spencer looked at the phone, then put it gently back on its cradle. It rang again and he said wearily, 'Spencer—'

There was a pause.

Spencer said, 'Answer, blast it!'

It was Frank. She said in a very hurt voice, 'I thought you'd be glad to hear from me ...'

Spencer said—

He sighed.


Conway Kan considered his bowl of jasmine tea. He looked worried. He said to O'Yee and the jasmine flower floating on the surface of the tea, 'May I ask if you have any thoughts on your method of procedure?' He looked very worried indeed.

O'Yee said, 'The—' He paused, 'The Ramphastes Toco is over a hundred years old?'

Conway Kan nodded. 'It was my father's. He was briefly in the Caribbean and preserved it as a reminder of those days.'

He said, 'He and my mother were married there.' He looked into the tea.

O'Yee said, 'I would assume that whoever took it would attempt to sell it. He said, 'The usual place for it to end up in that case would be an antique dealer's.' He said, 'If, as you say, there were no signs of forcible entry in your house, we can assume it was taken by someone who knew you.' He asked, 'No one would take it simply to hurt you?'

Conway Kan said, 'You are the first person to whom I have confessed its attachment for me.'

'Then I propose to get in touch with the dealers and see if it's been offered via a market stall or whatever.'

Conway Kan said, 'And the question of criminal charges?'

O'Yee said, 'It can remain a private matter. If you like, you simply have someone walk in and purchase the bird.'

Conway Kan nodded. He said, 'I fear you will lay yourself open to some ridicule asking people if they have bought a stuffed toucan.' He considered the meniscus in his cup.

O'Yee said, '*Te jen ch'ieh jen, te nai ch'ieh, nai.*'

'When it is proper to forbear, forbear.'

There was a silence.

O'Yee looked at Conway Kan. He looked like a very old man. Conway Kan looked down at the floor. There seemed to be tears in his eyes. He seemed to be a very long way away.

O'Yee said suddenly in English, 'For Christ's sake, don't worry! I'll fix it!' He thought, 'God, there goes a million dollars ...'

Conway Kan nodded. He seemed very embarrassed.

Conway Kan said, 'About this morning—' He said, 'I heard about – what happened with the men you found in the water and about—'

O'Yee nodded.

Conway Kan said, 'I know why you wanted to wait.' He said, 'I hear most things that happen in Hong Bay.' He said, 'I know what you were wondering about and whether or not you did the right thing about – about, you know—'

O'Yee nodded.

Conway Kan said, 'You were right to insist on recovering everything.' He said, 'The family of the man would be grateful if they knew.' He said, 'They will know.' He said, 'I shall see to it.'

O'Yee nodded and looked at the floor.

They sat in silence.

Feiffer and Auden watched Macarthur and the two ambulance-men put Mr Leung's body into an ambulance and take it away, then they went back into what was left of the ivory shop.

The ivory shop was a mess of ivory. It looked as though someone had taken a hammer to the two thousand small pieces of ivory Mr Leung had kept on his shelves and pounded each one of them to bits, then moved on with a large hammer to the larger pieces and pounded them as well. Feiffer went to the remains of Mr Leung's desk, blew a cloud of ivory dust from the surface, and bent down to sniff the black scorch mark in the centre of the wood. The wood smelled burnt. He glanced at the rear wall where Auden was bending down looking at something on the floor.

Auden said, 'Skin tissue.' He straightened up and looked at the third person in the room. The third person in the room, a man smoking a small black cigar, continued gathering up scraps of half-incinerated paper and slipping them into plastic bags with tweezers. He took his black cigar from his mouth, considered the length of its ash, opened a brown Gladstone bag near his feet, extracted a tiny silver ashtray, and ashed the ash in it. Auden said to him, 'Are you Forensic?'

The third person in the room shook his head. He smiled, closed the Gladstone bag and locked it. He found another scrap of paper and slipped it into a plastic bag.

The tearing-down of Yellowthread Street had halted briefly as a mark of respect. The third person in the room said 'Hmm . . .' to himself and picked up something metallic with his tweezers. He looked at it. It was part of a triggering device. The third person in the room looked at Feiffer.

Auden said to Feiffer, 'Who's he?'

Feiffer asked the third person in the room, 'Anything for us?' The third person in the room considered the triggering device and made a soft sniffing noise. He smiled at Auden. The third person in the room was one of those Chinese whose face seemed to have never seen a line or a wrinkle. His skin was very smooth: when he smiled his face was still expression-less.

He answered Feiffer, 'No.'

'It was a letter bomb though?'

'Yes.'

'Leung.'

'Yes.'

Feiffer said, 'The letter to us said political.' He asked the third person, 'Was he?'

'No.'

Auden asked Feiffer irritably, 'Who the hell is he?'

The third person in the room said to Feiffer, 'Why send a letter to the cops in advance if it's political? Why not just blow the bugger up without a word?'

Feiffer said, 'If you're thinking it's some sort of intimidation, forget it. If it's someone who didn't pay extortion to one of the local strong-arm men, they're still not going to tell us in advance.' He said, glancing at the ivory and the blood. 'Whoever sent the bomb intended it to go off.' He asked, 'Did you know him: Leung?'

'Did you?'

'Only by sight. We don't know anything against him. So far as I know at the moment he was exactly what he seemed to be, a middle aged Chinese male resident in Hong Bay who sold ivory.'

Auden said, 'Who the hell are you anyway?' He asked Feiffer, 'Is he a cop or what?'

The third person in the room said, 'I'll check up, but he's not a known political.' He said, 'If he is into something nasty it doesn't say much for my files.'

Auden said, 'You're Special Branch!'

Feiffer opened his notebook and flipped over a few pages.

'Have you got the wife's statement?'

Feiffer found the page.

Auden said, 'That's who you are! You're Special Branch!'

'*Mrs Leung, taken at scene of crime by Detective Chief Inspector* and so on.'

The third person in the room tapped the end of his cigar on the rim of the silver ashtray. The cigar was out. He unlocked his brown Gladstone bag and put the remains of the cigar and the half-filled ashtray into a little paper bag and placed it carefully somewhere in one of the leather pockets. He closed his bag again and locked it.

'"Who did it? I know who did it! It was him! He did it! Question: Who is 'him'?"'

Auden looked at the third person in the room. That was who he was all right. No doubt about it.

'"Tam! That's who did it! Tam! His so-called partner! Him! He said he would and he did! It was him!"'

Before they had taken the body away, Mrs Leung had shrieked, 'His so-called partner! His so-called rotten, lousy, vermin-infested friend! Him! Him with half the profits on his lousy bacteria-ridden capital and no work for the business! Him! That man! Mr plague-poxed Tam! Him! Him! Him! She had caught sight of one of her husband's bloodied hands under the plastic sheet the ambulancemen had used to cover him and shouted, 'My poor husband!' She shrieked, 'Who's going to support me and my children in my old age now?' She shrieked at Feiffer, 'It was him! Tam!'

Feiffer made a note in his notebook. He asked quietly, 'Address?'

'Soochow Street! Somewhere in a rat hole in Soochow Street! Somewhere where decent clean people—'

'This man Tam was your husband's partner?'

'It all goes to him now! All of it! All because of his miserable few lice-crawling dollars – his *investment*!' She shrieked at Feiffer and the bloody lump under the rubber sheet, 'What do I get? Nothing! Nothing! She shrieked, 'All because of that pariah Tam!' She shouted to the heavens, 'Twenty-two years he's had money in the business and what has he done except take the profits? Nothing!' She put her hands over her face and wailed, 'My poor children!' She wasn't a day under fifty-five. She shouted, 'I'll never have any children now!'

Feiffer said, 'Tam.' He underlined the name in his book.

'Tam!' Mrs Leung took a breath.

Feiffer said, 'I see.'

'That – that dirt! That dog's diarrhoea! That rat-turd! Tam! That pariah! That – that—' She found another word, 'That – that *leper*!'

Feiffer closed his notebook.

Auden looked at the third person in the room. Special Branch. Written all over him.

The third person in the room said to Feiffer, 'You can't say fairer than that.' He said to Auden, 'That's what's known as a good line in insults.'

Auden thought, 'Sir? I'm a Detective Inspector, maybe he ought to add "sir". She does a good line in insults, *sir*. Doesn't she? Huh, maybe.' Auden asked brusquely, 'What rank are you?'

The third man in the room said, 'Detective Chief Inspector. How about you?'

Auden shut up.

The third man considered his collection of artifacts from the envelope. He watched Feiffer return the notebook to the pocket of his coat, 'And that's the shot you're following?'

'Yes.'

The third man in the room nodded. 'I think you're right. I'll have our people run what's left of the bomb through, but it doesn't strike me as a political job.' He asked Feiffer, 'Then why say it was in a letter to the local fuzz?' He said, 'I'll have a news clamp put on it anyway just in case.'

Feiffer nodded. He said, 'You'll let me know?'

The third man nodded. Auden said, 'Excuse me, Chief Inspector—'

Feiffer said, 'This fellow Tam seems to be a sitter for it. The wife claims he put money into the business donkey's years ago – and he's been sitting back and taking half the profits ever since.'

'There's nothing illegal in that.'

'I wouldn't be too sure that's the way she looks at it.' He went on, 'I gather that Leung has been trying to buy out his interest for some time. The people in the neighbouring shop say there was some question of a legal action.' He asked the third man in the room, 'Was it a professional bomb? A good one?'

'Fair average quality.'

'Not professional?'

'I wouldn't have said so. But it's someone who knew how to make a letter bomb all right.'

Feiffer glanced around the room. 'But it doesn't go against your initial reaction that it could have been constructed by an amateur on a one-off basis?'

'No.' The third man agreed, 'I think Tam is your best lead.'

He stifled an involuntary yawn. 'Hard night.' He said, 'I've been waiting for something to come off at the docks for the last eight weeks.' He was about to say more, but changed his mind. He said, 'I'll leave it to you, Harry? OK?' He said, 'You'll probably have it all sewn up by tea-time.' He said for no apparent reason, 'Watercress sandwiches and pink gin and Darjeeling tea.'

Auden thought—

Feiffer stifled a yawn.

The third man asked, 'Am I being boring?'

'Misinformed.'

The third man asked innocently, 'You mean the British chappies in the Colonies don't have pink gin and watercress sandwiches for tiffin?' He tutted. 'Oh dear—'

Feiffer said wearily, 'I don't happen to be a Colonial. I was born here.' He said, 'Which is more than I can say for you.'

The third man said, 'Hmm, that's right. So you were. I've got it on file.'

'That doesn't surprise me in the least.'

The third man asked, 'When is Nicola due to have the baby?'

'Two or three weeks.'

'Do I get invited to the christening?' He asked, 'Who's going to be the godfather?'

'Christopher O'Yee.'

'Oh.' The third person asked Auden, 'How about you? Mr Auden, isn't it?'

Auden said awkwardly, 'Well, you usually only have one godfa—'

The third person said, 'I meant, are you the sort of British chappie who has watercress sandwiches and gin for tiffin?'

Auden glanced at Feiffer. He said without thinking, 'Well, actually—'

'Well, actually,' the third person said, 'Actually one doesn't drink gin at tiffin.'

Auden said, 'Well, yes—'

Feiffer said to the third person, 'Shut up, Humphrey.'

Auden said— He thought, *Humphrey?* He asked in a wide-eyed stare of utter awe and amazement, 'Are you Humphrey—?'

'Ho,' Feiffer said. He said to the third person in the room, 'Humphrey Ho is the local Special Branch man.'

Auden nodded. He had the feeling his mouth hung open. He said—

Humphrey Ho said, 'Humphrey Ho is the *only* Special Branch man.' Humphrey Ho said, 'Hong Bay Special Branch *is* Humphrey Ho.' He said, 'Humphrey Ho is—'

Feiffer went towards the door.

Humphrey Ho said again for his benefit, 'Humphrey Ho is—'

Feiffer paused. He looked at Auden's face. He said briskly to Auden, 'Come on. You're going back to the Station to type up your reports.'

The third person asked, 'Do you want Humphrey Ho to assist you in your arrest?'

'No.'

Humphrey Ho said, 'Humphrey Ho is willing.'

'Humphrey Ho can go back to his grimy little room and make out a report for me.'

'Humphrey Ho is not a man to be too much in love with form-filling,' Humphrey Ho said, 'Humphrey Ho is—'

Feiffer glanced at Auden. He said evenly, 'Humphrey Ho is a pain in the arse.' He said to Auden, 'Will you come on!'

Humphrey Ho's expressionless face fell. There was still no expression on it. He said quietly, 'Harry ...'

He seemed hurt.


Three quarters of an hour later Feiffer stood outside the door on the second floor of a run-down residential hotel in Soochow Street. There was a card on the door with three Chinese characters written on it. The card had been there a long time. The characters said, TAM WING KIN. The characters were a little blurred and dusty as if they, and the card, and possibly the man inside the door that held them, needed replacement.

Feiffer opened his coat and slipped the hammer retaining loop off the two-inch barrelled Colt in his holster.

He knocked on the door.


There were another two long manilla envelopes in the sorting racks of the Hong Bay Central Post Office in Wyang Street, but they would not be delivered, what with sorting, bagging, dividing, resorting, shuffling and rubberbanding, for another four hours.

A thin voice on the other side of the dusty card and the dusty characters said very softly, 'Please come in—' and Feiffer opened the door.

# 3

In the sorting room of the Hong Bay Central Post Office in Wyang Street, the Assistant Senior Chief Sorter, Mr Choy, flicked the last two letters from his pile into the pigeon-hole marked Yellowthread Street. The long manilla envelopes were addressed in black ink. One of them slipped out and fluttered back on to Mr Choy's sorting desk. It felt a little heavy. He slapped it back into the slot, nodded to his assistant, and went off to get his tea.

His assistant bagged the last two letters in the top of a canvas sack, secured the sack with a length of double looped string and pushed the sack on to the open steel chute that took the sacks direct to the postmen's room downstairs. The sack disappeared down the chute and, two floors below, hit the cement floor of the postmen's room with a thud.

There were one hundred and ten antique shops and dealers listed in the Yellow Pages of the Hong Kong Island telephone directory alone. The Hong Kong Island telephone directory alone was an inch and three quarters thick on thin paper. That still left the Kowloon and New Territories book. That was three inches thick. In the corridor of the Yellowthread Street Police Station, O'Yee sighed.

He took the interview room extension telephone into the interview room and then went back for the two phone books. He put the phone and the phone books on the plain table in the room, plugged the phone in, and sat down on one of the plain chairs to start ringing.

The sorting was a little behind time and the postmen were

waiting for the last bag so they could start their deliveries.

Feiffer paused at the open door. The room was semi-lit by a slate grey light coming in from an uncurtained window. There was a blurred figure sitting at a table by the window, looking out.

Feiffer said, 'Police.' There was an odd smell in the room.

The blurred figure at the table didn't move.

O'Yee rang the first antique dealer.

It was five past twelve in the afternoon.


Soochow Street forms the cross bar of the H stroke of General Gordon Street and Peking Road and runs parallel with Generalissimo Chen Street and the Government-run New Hong Bay Cemetery, which is still open for business.

Even closer to Soochow Street, not open for new business but closed in the late nineteen fifties, is the privately owned and maintained Double Tranquillity Resting Place of Heavenly Peace.

Midway between these two necropolises, in Empress of India Street, are the (Chinese) Government-run Communist Party offices, school and bookshops and, three doors down from them, the (now) privately run Nationalist Party offices, school and bookshops.

The two cemeteries promise prosperity, joy, happiness and beauty in the next world, the Communists promise it in this, and the Nationalists promise that really, for all the promises, it was all like that yesterday (only nobody knew it), and Soochow Street, which intersects, divides, straddles, locates and fixes these conflicting theses is (to borrow a Marxist dialectic) the synthesis of all the promises.

It stinks.

There is a death-house for old people at one end of it, and, at the other, another. All the views from the windows of the slums between the two death-houses at either end (the death-houses themselves are also slums) are of the cemeteries, and the only people who walk up and down Soochow Street are people waiting to die, people waiting for someone else to die, people who have just had someone die or would like to and people on their way to the dead in the cemeteries.

Soochow Street is a coffin open at both ends for the extinct, and it has that distinctive smell of death and extinction that is composed of coldness and greyness and mould. Soo-chow Street always looks as if there has just been rain and the wooden walls of the buildings on either side of it are always wet and clammy to the touch.

Moss grows there between the cracks in stone and paint-cracking timber. If ever one went back in time to a time al-ready past, the past would be the greyness of Soochow Street.

The odd smell was of something dying. The figure in the half light looked steadily out of the window. The grey picture out of the window that brought a little light into the darkened room was the cemetery. It was the smaller cemetery, the Double Tranquillity Resting Place of Heavenly Peace. Now closed.

'Mr Tam?'

The thin voice said, 'Yes.' There was nothing in it: no fear, surprise, a little interest.

Feiffer said in Cantonese, 'My name is Feiffer. I'm a Detec-tive Chief Inspector from the Yellowthread Street Station.' He tried to make out the facial features, but the room was too dim. From the way the neck bent forward, it was an old man.

The thin voice said, 'Yes?' There was another chair by the table. The thin voice said, 'Please.'

Feiffer sat down. The chair creaked. It had not been used for a very long time. Mr Tam said, 'Yes?'

'I believe you are a partner in the firm of Leung Ivory in Yellowthread Street?'

'The shop?' There was a soft sigh, 'Yes.'

Feiffer peered at the face. There was something odd about it. It was too dim to see. But there was something definitely odd about it. Feiffer said quietly, 'Mr Leung is dead.'

There was a pause. Feiffer asked, 'Did you hear what I said? Did you understand me?'

'Your Cantonese is very good.'

'Thank you. Did you understand what I said?'

There was another pause. The thin voice said, 'Yes.' There was a second soft hissing sound of breath.

'He was killed by an explosive device. A bomb' – there was no reaction – 'A letter bomb. Someone manufactured a letter bomb with gelignite and a detonator set to explode when it was opened.'

'Yes.'

Feiffer said, 'Was it you?'

The thin voice asked, 'Why should I wish to kill anyone?'

'Mr Leung was your financial partner.'

'No.' Whatever it was the eyes saw from the window, they did not deviate from it. The voice said again softly, 'No.'

'Mr Leung's widow claims you are.'

'I am not.'

'You have no connection with the business? When I asked you a moment ago you said yes.'

The figure made a slight movement. There was the strange smell again. 'Mr Leung was a financial partner in the sense that he took money from it on a percentage basis, but he was not, in the sense you mean, a full partner.'

Feiffer asked, 'Who owns the business?'

Mr Tam's voice said softly, 'I do.' He sounded very frail and tired.

'And Mr Leung was an employee?'

'Yes.'

'Then why would his widow claim he was a partner? All it would take from you is a word.'

The figure was silent.

'I see.'

The figure was silent.

'When was the last time you were in the shop, Mr Tam?'

Mr Tam said softly, 'I have not left this room for the last three years.' He said, 'I am provided for by the profits from the business.' He said softly, 'I have received nothing for three months now.'

Feiffer said—

The thin voice said, 'It doesn't matter.'

'Did you make the bomb?'

There was a strange note in the voice. The voice said, 'The cemetery is closed now, but there is a place reserved there for me.' The voice said, 'I used most of the profits to endow in a small way, an orphanage.' The voice said, 'So.'

'So there will be people to mourn you and tend your grave.'

The voice said, 'Yes.' There was a quickened note in the tone, 'Yes.' He said, 'The most important thing in life is to be buried properly.' He said, 'That is a Chinese view.'

'Yes, I know.'

Mr Tam said, 'I have not killed anyone. I have done a few

47

little things of merit and nothing much that is too bad.' He said, 'I am hopeful that my meritorious works will be enough.' He said sadly, 'I can do no more now in any event.'

Feiffer drew a breath. Something pushed against his ribs. It was the butt of his gun. He moved his hand down to the holster and slipped the retaining leather loop over the hammer to secure it. 'Mr Leung's widow seems to think you are a very evil man.'

Mr Tam did not reply.

Feiffer said, 'She claims you are a pariah.'

Mr Tam's head nodded.

Feiffer said, 'Plague-poxed.' He said, 'Dog's diarrhoea. Rat-turd. Leper. Vermin-infested.' He told the figure, 'She accused you over the body of her husband.' He asked, 'Have you any idea what gelignite does to a human body at close range?'

Mr Tam said, 'No.'

'She claims you and her husband were equal partners in the business and that you were content to sit back and take the profits while he put in the work. She feels that you will now take the entire business and her income will cease.' He said evenly, 'I think you'll admit that it makes a very convincing motive.'

The figure was still.

Feiffer said, 'Wouldn't you say so?'

The figure nodded. The thin voice said, 'She may have the business.'

'Pardon?'

'If she wants the business she may have it.' The thin voice said, 'It is of no use to me.' He said to Feiffer, 'Do you know what feng shui is?' He added quickly, 'Of course, you must.'

Feiffer said, 'Wind and water. They're supposed to be the propitious elements for a house or a grave, or whatever.'

The figure nodded.

Feiffer asked, 'How is the feng shui in that cemetery you can see?'

'It is the best in Hong Kong.' The figure said, 'The cemetery was built in the middle of the last century. It was one of the first on the island, so there were any number of sites to choose from.' He said, 'A feng shui diviner was brought from Canton to locate the best site.' He said, 'A tomb has belonged there to my family for generations. I am the last of my family to use it.'

He said, 'It will not be very long.' He said, 'I am waiting.'

*Did you make the bomb that killed Mr Leung?*

Mr Tam said, 'The last. I am one of the last. The cemetery has been closed for over twenty years and I am one of the very last.' He said, 'A man was brought all the way from Canton to divine the spot.' He said, 'I am one of the very last.' He said, 'I have been waiting for ten years, but it will be soon.' He said, 'They said on the island that it will be soon.' He told Feiffer, 'They brought me over.' He asked him, 'They wouldn't do that if it wasn't soon would they?' He reassured himself, 'No.'

'Which island?'

'Oh, the—' Mr Tam said, 'Hei Ling Chau Island.' Mr Tam said, 'A long time ago I used to carve ivory. I could have made something then.' He said, 'That was a long time ago.' Feiffer was very aware of the smell. He knew what it was. There was a silence.

The figure said, 'Mr Feiffer?'

'Yes.' Feiffer stood up. He went to the window. He could see the cemetery on its little hill, with its rows and rows of tombs set out like neat houses on an estate. On the other side of the hill was the harbour.

Mr Tam said, 'What do you think?'

'Yes.'

'Beautiful?'

Feiffer said, 'It's a fine place.'

'Yes.' Mr Tam said, 'Do you think I am an evil man?'

'No.'

Mr Tam said, 'If she wishes the business, Mr Leung's window may have it.' He asked, 'Will you put it in writing?'

'I will telephone someone for you.'

Mr Tam said, 'That would be an act of merit.'

Feiffer looked out at the cemetery. As far as he could see to the top of the hill, there were little grave markers. He asked, 'Where is your family's tomb?'

'On the other side of the hill.'

'Overlooking the water?'

'Yes.'

Feiffer said, 'The best feng shui is probably over there.'

Mr Tam said, 'It is.' He asked, 'Did I tell you a man was brought all the way from Canton to divine the site?'

'No.'

'It is true.' The smell was very strong.

Feiffer said, 'I'm sorry to have bothered you.' He said quietly, 'I envy you your place.'

Mr Tam said, 'There are no more places left.' He said, 'The New Government Cemetery is a good place, but it does not have the feng shui of this site.'

'No.'

Mr Tam said, 'I will not have to wait much longer.'

Feiffer nodded. He stood by the window looking out at Mr Tam's place for a long time until Mr Tam finally dozed off into an uneasy sleep, then he went quietly out of the room and shut the door softly behind him.

Leprosy is a disease that often takes up to thirty years to kill. Now known to be normally non-contagious in many forms, it is, nevertheless, in many ways, totally unpredictable. What is not totally unpredictable however are the parts of the body it attacks: the nose, eyebrows and limb extremities. These, often to the accompaniment of a pungent smell, become deadened and, apparently of their own accord, mortify and, finally, drop off. These symptoms are certain, as indeed, is the fact that, without fingers, it is very difficult to fabricate anything as delicate as a bomb.

Feiffer turned out of Soochow Street. A stream of taxis went by on their way back from the cross harbour tunnel, but he let them go by. He decided to walk back to the Station.

He stopped at the corner of Great Shanghai Road and Jade Road and lit a cigarette.

The first letter was addressed to a man named Wong. The postman handed it to him and then passed on down Yellowthread Street towards the Police Station. Apart from the dozens of other letters to be delivered on the way, he had a long manilla envelope to be dropped into the Detectives' Room at the Police Station.

The late sorting had put him behind time and he quickened his pace.

# 4

Mr Wong looked at his letter. A customer came up to his hot chestnut stall outside the Paradise Cinema on the corner of Canton Street and Yellowthread Street and proffered a ten cent coin. Mr Wong put the letter to one side next to his charcoal burner and filled a brown paper cornet from a metal scoop. The customer nodded. Mr Wong dropped the ten cents into his box and looked at the letter for the second time. Mr Wong thought about it for a moment. He scooped up his scoop, his money box and his letter and ran after the postman. He thought the letter must be a mistake. He never got letters. The few letters he had had in his forty-three years had been from the Government. They were always bad news: always something to pay. This one, though, was a mistake. Letters from the Government were always addressed in Chinese.

He caught the postman by the shoulder and tried to give him back the letter. The postman, in a hurry, refused to take it.

Mr Wong showed him the spidery black ink address. He said reasonably to the postman, 'It's in English.'

The postman said, 'So what?' There was a heavy pumice dust in the air and the postman coughed. Encouraged, a pneumatic drill on the fifth or sixth floor of one of the half torn down buildings coughed with him, then went BERAMABER-AMABRRAMA! A hammer started going BANG! BANG! BANG! The postman said, 'I can't wait around here, I've got work to do!' He looked at Mr Wong's eyes. They seemed very worried. The postman wasn't a hard man. He said, 'It's for you. It's got your name on it.' He took the letter and turned it over to show Mr Wong his name in the strange letters. He said, 'See?'

Mr Wong said, 'No.'

'*Wong.*'

Mr Wong said, 'It's not me.' He had troubles enough of his own without opening anyone else's. He said, 'It's the wrong Wong.' He nodded. He turned to go back to his chestnuts and an undisturbed life. He was glad that was over. The nail guns fired a volley or two, then the hardiest went POW! POW!

The postman stopped him. He handed the letter back. Mr Wong refused to take it. The postman said, 'Wong Tung Shing, right? That's you, isn't it? Street Vendor Number 5817, corner Yellowthread Street and Canton Street, Hong Bay.' He said, 'That's you, right? That's your location.' He warned Mr Wong. 'Don't tell me it isn't. I've seen you there every day for years.' He said with the power of his uniform and his Government job with a pension attached to it, 'That's you!' He pushed the letter into Mr Wong's hands and crushed the corners of the stamp.

Mr Wong said, 'It isn't mine!' He tried to give it back.

'It's yours!' The postman shoved his shoulder to move him along.

'Well, I can't read it!'

'That's not my problem!'

Mr Wong said, 'You read it to me!'

The postman looked at him. His mouth said in silent horror at the suggestion that he should demean his position, 'Haw!' He told Mr Wong in a scandalized voice, 'I'm not employed to read letters to illiterates!'

'I'm not illiterate! I don't read English! That doesn't make me illiterate!' He demanded from the postman, 'Do you read Arabic?'

'Of course not!'

'Well, I do!'

The postman paused. He asked, 'Do you?'

Mr Wong said, 'Well – no.' He asked quietly, 'Would you mind reading it for me?'

The postman glanced at his watch. He hesitated. He took the envelope back and gazed at it. He said quietly, 'Look, I'm sure it isn't bad news.' He indicated the handwritten address, 'It isn't from the Government.' He said, 'The Government wouldn't employ anyone with such bad handwriting. And they're always written on a typewriter.' He said, 'They always have a return address to the Government Office.' Mr Wong looked impressed. The postman added, 'And they never have a stamp on them because Government letters don't need one.' He said with the final crushing deductive powers of a Sherlock Holmes, 'So it isn't from the Government.'

Mr Wong said, 'Oh ...' So that was what it took to get a Government job. Mr Wong said humbly, 'I'm very impressed.' (The postman made a deprecating move of his head.) He could see why a man like this wouldn't have the time to stop to read other people's letters. He said, 'I'll take the letter to a letter-writer at the Post Office.' He said firmly to show he had taken the point, 'It's their business to read letters in other languages, not yours.'

The postman wasn't a hard man. He said, 'Nor yours either.' He said, 'You've got your own business to think of. You haven't the time to run about learning languages you never use.' He smiled and hoisted his bag higher on his shoulder.

Mr Wong nodded. There was a letter-writer he knew vaguely in Wyang Street just outside the Post Office who wasn't such a bad sort. And there was always the indisputable fact that letter-writers would probably read letters (as opposed to writing them) for a discount. He said decisively to the postman, 'I'll take it to a letter-writer.'

The postman nodded. That was the ticket. Mr Wong smiled and went to close up his chestnut stall. The postman thought he would be all right for a few hot chestnuts from now on. He hoisted his bag and went on his way. The story that had gone around was that Leung's shop had been blasted by a gas explosion from a leaking pipe in the basement.

The postman smiled. No one had told him he was in the bomb-delivering business.


The voice at the other end of the line said, 'Hong Bay Fine Arts shop—'

O'Yee drew a line through their entry in the phone book. 'Good afternoon.'

'Good afternoon, sir.'

O'Yee drew a breath. This was the third. He was getting tired of cultured voices. He said in English, 'I wonder if you can help me?'

The voice at the other end of the line caught its breath. The catch in the breath said, 'Here's a live one.' The voice said hopefully in English, 'Are you an American gentleman, sir?' The voice was already calculating the exchange rate.

O'Yee said, 'Yes.'

'Ah,' the voice said, 'How may I be permitted to assist you?'

'Stuffed birds.'

There was a brief pause. 'Quite,' the voice said. It said, 'Ha, ha.' (It was some sort of American joke.) The voice said, 'Yes – ha, ha.'

'Do you have any?'

'Any what?'

'Any stuffed birds?'

'No, sir—' The voice said, 'Ha, ha.'

'Ha, ha,' O'Yee said. 'Goodbye.'

He hung up.

The next listing was for the Hong Bay Fine Arts *Company*. Maybe it was the same gang. O'Yee dialled the number. Another cultured voice (how many Cantonese elocution schools were there?) said, 'Hong Bay Fine Arts *Company*.'

'Any connection with the Hong Bay Fine Arts *Shop*?'

'Oh, no, sir—!'

'Any stuffed birds?'

'Oh, no, sir—!'

He hung up.

Spencer was reading a roneoed brochure put out by the Home Office in London entitled *The Layman's Guide to Letter Bombs*. He turned the page from the ounce to injury ratios to the section on how to dismantle the things. He didn't much like the sound of it. There was an X-ray photo of a percussion activated example and he turned the picture around to study it from another angle.

Constable Sun came in and tossed a single letter on his desk. It was addressed to Feiffer. Spencer said, 'He's out on a job.'

Sun nodded. He went out the door and back down the corridor to his front desk.

Spencer turned the X-ray picture another way to get a better look at the trigger mechanism. He thought since the boss was out he had better see if the letter was important. He put it to one side of his desk, turned the picture to yet another angle, and opened the top drawer of his desk to get a letter opener.

The single sheet of paper in the brown envelope said, *Wong. Political.* There was nothing else.

A cultured voice, 'Hong Bay Treasures and—'

'Stuffed birds!'

'What?'

'STUFFED BIRDS!'

'NO!'

'GOOD!'
'IT'S A PLEASURE!'
'THANK YOU!'
'GO TO HELL!'
He hung up.

'Do you mean *dead* birds? *Dead* ones?'
'Yes, I mean dead ones!'
A cultured voice said, 'Yech!'
The line went, like the birds, dead.

Auden wrenched open the telephone book. He found the list-
ing for *Wong*. There were thousands of them. He asked
Spencer, 'First name?'
'It's not here!'
'What do you mean, it's not there?'
Spencer shoved the paper around with the end of a pencil.
'It just says *Wong!*'
Auden came over and glanced at it. He looked up at
Spencer. Spencer said, 'I don't know!' He looked at the clock.
The seconds were ticking away.
'Which one?' Auden looked back at the telephone book
desperately. 'Which one?' He demanded from the clock,
'Which one?' He shouted at Spencer, '*Which bloody Wong?*'

O'Yee thought, 'This is a hell of a life.' He marked off the
next entry in the directory and began dialling the number. He
waited for the next cultured, fruity male voice to say, 'Good
morning, may I help you?' and then inform him that never,
never, never would they handle anything as uncultured, unfruity, unsuave and generally totally disgusting as a stuffed
bird.
The voice at the other end of the line was a female one. Her
tone was like the chimes of a faraway temple bell on a cool
evening.
She informed him that never, never, never would they handle
anything as uncultured, unfruity, unsuave and generally totally
disgusting as a stuffed bird.
But she did it in an extremely nice way.

Auden said, 'I'll ring Humphrey Ho!' He dialled the number

and got a recorded female voice. The recorded voice said, 'The subscriber to this number is out. Please check that you have dialled the number you require. You have in all probability dialled the wrong number.' The voice said, 'Should you dial again and find you have this number correctly, you may then leave a message after the tone.' The voice said, 'Please dial your number within sixty seconds.'

Auden hesitated. He dialled again. He expected, this time, Ho would answer.

The recorded female voice said, 'You may now leave your message.'

Auden hung up. He pushed the letter around on Spencer's desk with his pen to keep his fingerprints off it. The letter said :

*Wong. Political.*

And not one lousy, goddamned stinking syllable more!

Nicola Feiffer was on the phone to Emily O'Yee. She said miserably, 'No.'

'Not even a slow-moving tortoise?'

'Not even a non-ambulatory gnat!' She said, 'It's the lease.' She asked Emily, 'Isn't yours the same?'

'Probably.' Emily O'Yee thought of the three forces of doom, desolation and domestic destruction that masqueraded as her children. She said, 'The question of having a pet hasn't ever come up.' She said, 'There must be something clever you can get to keep you company that doesn't contravene the lease.'

'Hmm,' Nicola said. She said, 'Yes, there must be.'

Emily O'Yee said cheerfully, 'Let's think about it.'

Feiffer crossed over Stamford Road past the diamond merchants' area into Hanford Road. On the corner of Market Lane there was a fish restaurant called the Hong Bay Heavenly Cookhouse. He glanced up to the second floor where Ho had his office. The curtains were pulled. He went on towards the Jasmine Steps to cut into Wyang Street, thinking about Leung.

He thought, 'Surely it isn't possible that Leung's widow sent the bomb herself?' He thought, 'That's not normally the way wives kill their husbands.' He thought, 'And you don't just buy a copy of Teach Yourself Bomb-Making and whip up a letter bomb.' He thought, 'No.' He wondered what to do next. He thought, 'She must have known Tam was a leper. She must have known that Hei Ling Chau used to be a leprosarium.' He thought, 'No. It wasn't her.' He asked himself, 'Then who?' He wondered if Ho had come up with anything on the political side. He thought, 'Surely to Christ it wasn't just some maniac with a few ounces of gelignite who decided to try it out on the first person he thought of?'

He reached the entrance to the Jasmine Steps and thought, 'No, no one's that crazy.'

He thought, 'Yes, they are.'

O'Yee's eyes hurt. He put on his reading glasses and drew a line in black ink through the Hong Bay Antique Joys Emporium. He looked at the next entry. It was for the Hong Bay Celestial Treasures Company.

He sighed and dialled their number.

The letter-writer was an Indian from Johore Bahru in Malaysia named Ramaswamy. He was in his mid-forties like Mr Wong, and like Mr Wong, his name meant the equivalent of Smith. Mr Wong said, 'Mr Ramaswamy.'

Mr Ramaswamy said, 'Mr Wong.' He said, 'Ahaaa.' (It sounded like a horse whinny.) He adjusted his pens and pencils on his rickety wooden table outside the main entrance to the Post Office and said again, 'Ahaaa.'

Mr Wong said, 'I've got a letter.'

Mr Ramaswamy said, 'Ahaaaa, you mean that you *want* a letter.'

'No, I've *got* a letter.'

Mr Ramaswamy was not a man to be easily dissuaded from the habits or conversation of a lifetime. He asked, 'Who is it to go to?'

Mr Wong said, 'It's to go to me.' Obviously, this man Ramaswamy was an idiot.

Mr Ramaswamy said, 'That's a bit odd, isn't it?' Clearly, this man Wong was a bit simple. He thought, 'You can't expect much from a Chinese.'

Mr Wong thought, 'You can't expect wonders from an Indian.' He thought, 'They're all thick.' He said, 'It isn't odd. The letter is addressed to me.'

Mr Ramaswamy said, 'You don't get a discount for dictating letters to yourself.' He said nervously, 'Ahaa.' He hoped the man wouldn't turn violent. He said, 'My rates, like the Ganges, are constant.'

Mr Wong said, 'I thought the Ganges flooded and then went dry?'

If there was one thing Mr Ramaswamy didn't like it was a funny Chinese. He said, 'The Ganges may, but I do not.' He thought, 'Take that!'

Mr Wong said, 'I received a letter that I can't read without my glasses. I want someone who has glasses to read it to me.'

'Oh—!' Mr Ramaswamy said. He said, 'Ahaaa – oh!'

Mr Wong said, 'I can't find my glasses, you see.' No need to admit you couldn't read Arabic to anything as low as an Indian. He said, 'Hmm.'

'Ah,' Mr Ramaswamy said. He thought, 'Here it comes again: the old Chinese face-saving trick.' He thought, 'Illiterate Chink.' He said, smiling, 'Oh – ah . . .'

Mr Wong said, 'It's in English.'

Mr Ramaswamy said, 'The price is the same.'

'The same as what?'

Mr Ramaswamy said, 'The price for reading letters is the same as the price for writing them.' He said, 'Foreign languages extra.'

Mr Wong said, 'English isn't a foreign language!' He said, 'Almost everyone speaks it!'

Mr Ramaswamy asked, 'Do you?' He shook his head, 'Foreign languages extra.' He said. 'Chinese too.'

'Chinese isn't a foreign language!'

'It is to me.' Mr Ramaswamy said, 'My native tongue is an extremely obscure Punjabi dialect.'

Mr Wong said, 'Who the hell speaks an extremely obscure Punjabi dialect outside the Punjab?'

Mr Ramaswamy said, 'Hardly anyone.' He smiled. He asked pleasantly, 'Have you got the letter?'

Mr Wong looked at him. God, he hated Indians! He asked, 'How much?' He kept the letter out of sight in his pocket.

Mr Ramaswamy sighed. God, he hated Chinks! He said, 'Same price.'

'The same as what?'

'The same price as writing them.'

Mr Wong decided to get furious. He demanded furiously, 'How much is that?'

Mr Ramaswamy said, 'It depends on the length.' He asked, 'How long is it?'

'I haven't opened it yet!'

'Why not?'

'Because I can't read it!'

Mr Ramaswamy smiled an evil smile. He said, 'I thought you said you'd lost your glasses?'

Mr Wong smiled back an equally evil smile (it was so evil it verged on the positively diabolical). He said, 'That's why I can't read it.'

Mr Ramaswamy said innocently, 'Then how did you know it's for you?'

'I know it's for me because the postman told me it was for me!'

'Oh,' Mr Ramaswamy said, 'Oh.' He said, 'He must have been wearing *his* glasses. Aye?'

Mr Wong said, 'My postman doesn't happen to *need* glasses!'

'Ahaaaa!' Mr Ramaswamy whinnied. Really, these low-life Chinks were no competition for a good brain trained in the philosophical air of the sub-continent. He said, 'His customers do.'

'I lost my glasses!'

Mr Ramaswamy said, 'Perhaps you could get the postman to look for them for you.'

Mr Wong wrenched the letter from his pocket and thrust it at Mr Ramaswamy. Mr Ramaswamy went to take it. Mr Wong thrust it away again. Mr Wong said, 'I want an estimate!'

Didn't they all? Mr Ramaswamy said, 'Estimates twenty cents.'

Mr Wong said, 'Estimates are free!'

Mr Ramaswamy said, 'Fifteen cents.'

'Nothing!'

Mr Ramaswamy said, 'Since I'm in a good mood and you've lost your glasses and you're obviously getting on in years, I'll make it ten cents.'

'Two cents!'

Mr Ramaswamy said, 'Ahaaaa!' That was a funny one.

Mr Wong said, 'Five cents and that's my best offer!'

Mr Ramaswamy said, 'I'll take it.' He took the letter and slit open the flap with his imitation Gurkha paper-knife.

Feiffer saw the flash. There was a brilliant white glare radiating out from a tiny pin point in front of the Post Office and a sudden single note of high static as the air around the pinhole was wrenched violently aside. Then there was a sound like a very loud pistol shot or a huge chain snapping and then the concussion roared down the street and blew people walking along the pavement to their knees.

There was a puff of grey smoke, then a heavy black cloud of smoke, then a rushing noise as the air raced back in to fill the vacuum. Something came floating down from around the Post Office like shotgun wads and there was something black and liquid against the wall of the building, flowing back down to the street. A woman began screaming, then another and another, and then there was the shattering wailing of a child suddenly filling its lungs with air, going red in the face with the strain of holding the full lungs tight, then letting go in an earsplitting single-note shriek.

Feiffer reached the Post Office. There was paper fluttering down and ink spread out on the pavement and flowing down the walls. Parts of it weren't ink. They were thicker than ink. There was a middle-aged Chinese in an apron standing by a splintered wooden table looking up at the ink on the wall. The Chinese looked like a stall owner or a chestnut seller. He seemed familiar. The ink and blood dribbled down the wall. It looked as though there was some sort of terrible carnivorous plant inside the pores of the bricks that had been terribly and deeply wounded pouring blood out through the cavities in the mortar.

There was something else against the wall, like an old blanket. It was someone dead. It slumped suddenly down from against the wall and one of the legs scrabbled against the pavement to run away. The scrabbling stopped. The old blanket fell full-length on to the pavement and lay looking up at the ink and blood coming down the wall.

There was the smell of something burning.

Then the smell stopped.

The dead blanket's head rolled to one side on the pavement. The eyes were open. They stared at the Chinese in the apron. The mouth fell open and the face continued to stare at the Chinese in the apron with its mouth about to form a single word.

The dead eyes continued to stare at the middle-aged Chinese in the apron. The mouth seemed to say, 'You—'

The middle-aged Chinese in the apron began screaming.

# 5

Mr Wong watched the ambulance taking the letter-writer's body away until it went around the corner of Wyang Street into Beach Road. It halted for a moment at the intersection, was lost in the stream of traffic, reappearing turning, and then was gone. No one on the scene had bothered to close the open eyes and he saw them staring upwards from under the rubber sheet, trying to make out where he was. Mr Wong swallowed. Someone had given him an American cigarette without a filter (and lit it for him; his lips were numb and unfeeling) and he drew on it not tasting the smoke. His fingers trembled. He took the cigarette out of his mouth. The end of it tasted like salt. There were two policemen keeping the crowd back outside the main door of the Post Office. They looked at him. He tried to stop his fingers trembling. There was a tall man with a Roman nose bending over a spot of blood with two detectives and pointing at something with some sort of metal instrument. The tall man had a cigarette in his mouth as well. It smelled pungent. Mr Wong glanced at his own cigarette. It wasn't American at all, but French. The tall man must have stuck it in his mouth and lit it for him. Mr Wong wondered how expensive French cigarettes must be in Hong Kong. He felt touched. He felt like crying. Someone called the tall man Doctor Macarthur.

Feiffer, Auden and Macarthur straightened up from the splash of blood on the pavement and wall. One of the police photographers took a photograph using a flash gun and waited to see if any more were required. Feiffer shook his head and the man went back to one of the police cars ejecting the flash-bulb as he went. It made a popping sound.

Doctor Macarthur said, 'You'd better get that man to a hospital.' He looked at Wong.

'I'd like to talk to him first.' That was a tall man wearing a stained white suit. Mr Wong wondered who he was. The tall man wearing the white suit wasn't smoking. Neither was the other one – a younger man with a tight, aggressive face.

Doctor Macarthur nodded. There was a second ambulance waiting by the photographer's police car and Doctor Macarthur looked at it significantly.

The man in the stained white suit came over to Mr Wong. Mr Wong looked at one of the Chinese policemen in the crowd. The man in the stained white suit said to Mr Wong in perfect Cantonese, 'Mr Wong, my name is Feiffer. I'm a police officer. I'd like to ask you a few questions if you're up to it.' Mr Wong's French cigarette had gone out and the police officer lit it for him with a black lighter.

Mr Wong nodded. He said, 'Mr—?' It was funny how he couldn't taste the cigarette.

'Feiffer.'

'Yes.'

Feiffer said, 'The letter was addressed to you and you brought it around here to be read?'

Mr Wong said, 'I lost my glasses.' He said, 'I don't wear glasses. I can't read English.'

Feiffer nodded. He asked, 'Which political party do you belong to?'

Which one? How many were there? Were there any? Mr Wong said, 'I—' He asked, 'Party?' He said, 'I don't understand.' The second detective – the one with the hard face – came up and stood next to the first one.

The man in the stained white suit said, 'Who would want to kill you, Mr Wong?'

'Me?'

'Yes.'

Mr Wong said, 'No—' He said, 'No, it was—' He said, 'No one would want to kill *me*—' He thought, 'It was meant for me!' He said, 'I thought it was meant for—' He thought, 'How would anyone know I would have taken it to a letter—' He said loudly, 'It was meant for me!'

Feiffer said to the one with the hard face, 'We did get a letter?'

Auden nodded.

Feiffer said, 'Mr Wong, do you know anyone who has a knowledge of explosives? Anyone at all?'

Mr Wong said, 'Oh, no!' It had been meant for him. He said, 'Oh, no!!' The cigarette dropped from his hand. His hand began trembling. He could not control his lips. He said, 'Oh, no! Oh no!!'

'Explosives!'

Mr Wong said, 'My brother! Only my brother! He works in Wharf Cove quarry!' He said, 'Oh no!!' He had a picture of the dead eyes trying to stare up through the rubber sheet. There was blood and tissue all over the wall and on the pavement. He said, 'Oh no!! OH NO!!'

The man in the white suit grabbed him. He took him by the shoulder or the arm. He held him somewhere. He grabbed him. Mr Wong knew he – the man in the white suit shouted (was he shouting?) – the man in the white suit's mouth was moving and there were loud words coming out (were they from him? Who had given him the cigarette? He—). The man in the white suit shouted, 'Explosives!' (Maybe it was his own voice.) Someone's voice said, 'Me! It was meant for me!' Someone's voice said, 'Not my brother! He wouldn't – it was meant for me!!' Mr Wong was aware of a loud hiccupping sound. It went up and up like an engine running out of control. There was quick breathing, getting louder. Someone said, 'Explosives!'

Mr Wong felt his shoulders lifting up and down. His shoulders were breathing. They were drowning. They were running out of breath. He couldn't see anything. His eyes were open but they couldn't see anything. He was under a rubber sheet. A sheet. A rubber sheet trying to force his eyes to look out through the rubber sheet and— He shouted, 'OH NO! OH NO! *OH NO!!*'

A voice said, 'That's it! No more!'

He was in an ambulance lying down and the man with the Roman nose was bending over him and talking softly to him about something. The man with the Roman nose had a black bag on a little table next to him. There were words on the bag. Mr Wong looked at him. Mr Wong said, 'I dropped your cigarette.' He felt like crying. He was very, very sorry about the waste. He said, 'I didn't mean to, but I dropped it.' He looked at the man's eyes.

The man nodded. He didn't seem to mind. The man with the Roman nose said, 'Here,' and gave him another cigarette, already lit.

Mr Wong was grateful. He started crying.

Outside, in the street, the last of the day shift of hammers, drillers, nail gunners and assorted noise-makers finished up and, until the evening shift came to take over, there was peace. Feiffer had the Wong letter in front of him on his desk, sealed in a clear plastic bag ready to go to Forensic. He touched it with the end of a pencil and the bag slid frictionlessly across the desk and stopped at the natural obstruction of a dog-eared and furry sheet of Government blotting-paper. He was on the other end of Feiffer's telephone. Feiffer listened. Ho said, 'It was polar ammon gelignite, between two and three ounces activated by a switch trigger held back by a spring loaded wire catch.' He made a grunting noise as he considered something. He said, 'It wasn't a professional job.'

Feiffer said, 'It seemed to work well enough.'

'Professional in the—'

Feiffer said, 'Yes?'

Ho paused. 'In the, um, terrorist sense.' He said quickly in his special Special Branch voice, 'I'm not saying we've had any experience of letter bombs on a terrorist basis in Hong Kong.' (Feiffer said, 'No.') 'But if we had had then the bomb sent to Leung's ivory shop would come as rather a disappointment.' He added quickly, 'I mean, in the professional sense.'

Feiffer said, 'Hmm.'

There was a brief pause. Ho said, 'I gather you were a witness to the second one.'

'You make it sound uncomfortably like you think it's the latest in a long line.'

'Unless you've got any leads.' Ho asked, 'Have you got any?'

Feiffer asked, 'Have you any ideas about the explosives? Where they might have come from? I mean, are they military or—'

'Commercial. It's a commercial blend.' Ho said, 'The batch numbers were totally obliterated so it's no use trying to distributors, but I can say that it's a fairly new consignment. It's a new brand that's only been available here for the last two months or so – no more at any rate.' He said exploratorily, 'Does that tie in with your lead?'

'What lead?'

'The one you haven't mentioned.'

Feiffer said, 'I assume by your interest in my lead that there's nothing in this job for you?'

'There's nothing in it for us.'

'It's not political?'

'No.' Ho said, 'Do you want to hear a totally unconvincing theory? It's the Triad secret societies paying off old scores or, on the other hand, it's the Triad secret societies extorting money from small businesses.' He said evenly, 'You have to admit that selling hot chestnuts on a street corner is a small business.'

'They don't come much smaller.' Feiffer said, 'It is a totally unconvincing theory.'

Ho said, 'It's the Commander's.'

'It sounds like it.' Feiffer asked, 'Is he overseeing the case on the official level?'

'No. We are. Special Branch. That keeps it all nice and clandestine. The official story is that the letter-writer was killed by an exploding Tilley lantern – you know, paraffin under pressure – so the news clamp still holds.' He said, 'Hang on while I light a cigar.'

Feiffer said, 'And adjust your cloak.'

'And adjust my cloak.' Ho said, 'Hang on a moment.' There was a pause. (Feiffer heard someone say, 'No, I wouldn't mention that ...' and then someone else, farther away say, 'I agree ...') and then Ho was back on the line. Ho made a breath exhalation too close to the phone for it to be real and said, 'That's better – I gather one of your people tried to ring me just before the second bomb went off. Is that true?'

Feiffer glanced at Auden. Auden was listening to the conversation with awestruck eyes (and, presumably, ears). Feiffer said, 'Where the hell were you anyway?'

Ho said, 'I also gather from my spies, eavesdroppers, informants and general busybodies that he wanted to ask me which Wong was about to be blown to pieces.' He said, 'You might ask him just what the hell would make him think I might know.' He added, 'And then you might run him around to an advanced Cantonese course at the Government Language School to fix it in his little English brain just how many Wongs there are in this part of the world.' He said irritably, 'You might say I'm a little bit annoyed about it, Harry.'

Feiffer glanced at Auden. He was listening. Feiffer said, 'You don't expect me to take that comment seriously, do you?'

'Certainly I do!'

'Then you ought to get someone to run you around to Dale Carnegie's and get it into your little Special Branch pointy ears that senior officers don't let other senior officers tell them how to treat their junior officers.' He said to fix the point, 'Chief Inspector.'

At the other end of the line, Ho paused. Feiffer heard him say something to whoever else it was in his room above the restaurant in Stamford Street. Ho said, 'It must have been pretty unpleasant seeing someone blown to bits against a brick wall.'

Feiffer said, 'It was.'

Ho asked, 'What's your lead?' He said, 'I hope it's a better one than the one you had to that poor bastard Tam in Soochow Street.' He asked, 'Is it to a quarry or something? Does that explain the sudden interest in explosives?'

Feiffer asked, 'Why *political* in his letters if it isn't?'

Ho did not reply.

Feiffer said, 'Why tell us at all?' He said, 'I've sent Bill Spencer around to the Central Post Office in Wyang Street to intercept anything funny that might turn up in the evening collections, but that one beats me.' He said cautiously, 'No one telegraphs their punches unless they intend to use it as a feint.' He said to Ho, 'That is, assuming they know what they're doing.'

'You mean in relation to the construction of the bombs?'

'Well?'

Ho said, 'Well, they're not that bad. Not professional, but certainly an inspired amateur.' He said, 'And they work, don't they?' He asked again, 'Tell me your lead. I could do with the glory of swiping your arrest.' He said mock-reverently, 'Chief Inspector.' He said, 'Cheer up, the Commander will be on to you in the next – I estimate twenty minutes.' He said, 'Chief Inspector Sahib—'

Feiffer hung up and glared at Auden. Auden looked away. The letter had come to rest against the blotting-paper face down. The back of the page was blank.

*Wong. Political.*

Feiffer turned the plastic bag over with his pencil. That was all it said.

*Wong.*

Feiffer shook his head. He stared at the words.

*Political.*

He said aloud to the page, 'Why?'

It made no sense at all.

*Why?*

O'Yee was in a temper. He snarled into the black, evil, rotten, ill-mannered, lousy telephone in the interview room, 'Hullo!'

There was a pause. A voice said pleasantly, 'Hong Bay Antiquities and Ancient Treasures of Delight.' It faded away on a soft musical piano note. 'Mr Ting, sole proprietor and owner at your disposal, late of the Fine Art Saleroom of the illustrious enterprise of Burrard, Wu & Son. May I ask the name of the worthy gentleman who deigns to condescend to patronize my small but quality establishment?' There wasn't the faintest trace of irony. Mr Ting said respectfully, 'Sir?'

O'Yee felt as if a typhoon had suddenly been taken away from his spinnaker without even so much as a noticeable flutter. He said, 'Oh. Oh, yes.' He said, 'My name is O'Yee.'

'Mr O'Yee—!' It sounded like it had made Mr Ting's day. He asked, 'How, sir, may I assist you?' (O'Yee thought, 'This is a bit more like it.') Mr Ting inquired softly, 'Is there some small service I may have the honour of doing for your good self?'

O'Yee said, 'Oh.' He said, 'Mr Ting.'

Mr Ting said, 'Late of the illustrious firm of Burrard, Wu & Son, Mr O'Yee, where I did the few unimportant tasks alloted me to the best of my poor ability.'

O'Yee swallowed. He felt very guilty.

Mr Ting said, 'Fortunate though I was to thriftily amass sufficient capital to establish my own unworthy competition to them, I feel my little premises in no way compares to theirs.' He waited.

O'Yee said, 'I'm sure your establishment is much nicer all round.'

Mr Ting said, 'Thank you, sir.' He sounded like a humble heterosexual tailor forced to accept the task of measuring inside legs, 'I fear you are much too generous in your praise, but thank you.' He said gratefully, 'My dear sir.'

O'Yee said, 'I fear my praise may not even begin to be adequate.'

'My dear sir—' No, that was really too much . . .

O'Yee said, 'Mr Ting—'

'My dear sir—'

'Mr Ting—'

'Yes, my dear sir—'

'I have a small inquiry—'

'At your service.' (O'Yee waited) Mr Ting said, '—my dear sir.'

O'Yee said, 'I'm a rather discerning collector of taxidermed feathered vetrebrate fauna. I thought perhaps you might—'

Mr Ting said, 'My dear sir, I am at your every whim.' He repeated thoughtfully, 'Feathered vertebrate fauna.' He was working it out.

O'Yee said, 'Yes.'

Mr Ting worked it out. He said, 'Ah.'

'Ah.'

Mr Ting said, 'Perhaps a rather lovely and exquisite jade treasure of great antiquity representing the mythological bird of—'

O'Yee said, 'Taxidermed.' He said, 'Stuffed.'

There was a pause. Mr Ting said, 'I beg sir's pardon?'

O'Yee said, 'A stuffed bird. A toucan. A stuffed toucan.' He waited for Mr Ting to draw in his breath and say, 'My dear sir—!'

Mr Ting, at the other end of the line, drew in his breath.

O'Yee glanced at the blank apple-green ceiling of the interview room.

Mr Ting said, 'What?'

O'Yee forced a half-smile. It was a difficult thing to force. He said soothingly to Mr Ting without a trace of irony in his voice, 'Mr Ting— My dear sir—'

Mr Ting said, 'What?'

'People do collect stuffed birds, you know! I mean, just as many people collect stuffed birds as people collect jade treasures of great antiquity representing the—'

Mr Ting said, *'What?'*

'Have you got any bloody stuffed toucans for sale? Yes or no?'

Mr Ting said, 'WHAT?'

'Stuffed goddamned bloody dead extinct stuffed lousy toucans! Yes or bloody no?'

Mr Ting said, 'No!'

O'Yee said, 'Well, thank you very much! I'm dreadfully sorry I disturbed you!'

There was a terrible pause, then, after a long while, there was Mr Ting's voice back on the line. It had a lost, wounded note to it, like a Walt Disney Bambi wasting away in the forest with its great brown eyes raising themselves with aching tenderness to the memory of Cinderella or Mary Poppins or Marcus Welby (it was all in there). Mr Ting said utterly sadly, 'Oh . . .' Mr Ting said, 'Oh my dear sir . . .'

Mr Ting let out a single, long sigh. He said, very softly, 'Thank you . . . my dear sir . . .' and then, barely perceptibly, let the line go dead.

In the empty interview room O'Yee took off his glasses and wiped them with his handkerchief. He looked at them and swallowed. His identity, at once, reflected back at him twofold in the lenses, became forever and finally, irrevocably clear to him.

O'Yee was the man who, in front of his own children, in the final scene of the very last reel, had shot Lassie.

In the sorting room of the Hong Bay Central Post Office in Wyang Street, the Assistant Chief Senior Sorter, Mr Choy, looked at his branch Postmaster and said incredulously, *'Bombs? Letter bombs?'*

The branch Postmaster, Mr Hwang, nodded. He looked very nervous. He jerked his head significantly to the fair-haired European standing next to him. Mr Hwang said, 'This is Detective Inspector Spencer. If you suspect anything, leave it alone and call him.' He asked Mr Choy, 'Is that perfectly clear?' Mr Hwang said warningly to Spencer, 'I don't want any accident.' He surveyed the sorting booths, the canvas bags, the steel chute, the roof, the floor, the walls, the personnel (with a little less concern), the – he surveyed everything in the Hong Bay Central Post Office that belonged to the Hong Bay Central Post Office and felt responsible. He said to Spencer, 'I hold you responsible.' He nodded. He went back to his office, shaking his head.

Mr Choy watched him for a moment. Mr Hwang's office door opened and Mr Hwang went in. Mr Choy said, 'Don't mind him.' He offered Spencer a cigarette.

Two floors below, at the unloading dock, the evening's collections were arriving in canvas bags and being sent upstairs on conveyor belts to be sorted. It was 6 p.m.

Spencer took out a photostat of the bomber's handwriting from the inside pocket of his coat. He examined it. The first canvas bag reached the top of the conveyor belt and was hurled in the direction of a sorting table by one of the junior mail officers.

It went crash! on to the steel-topped surface.


The Wharf Cove granite quarry, set back from Hong Bay Beach Road on the western side of the district, was lit by a battery of floodlights. Feiffer pulled his car up to the padlocked wire gate entrance and glanced at his watch in the glow. It was 7.15 p.m. He locked his car door and went up to the gate. There was a guard dog on patrol around a group of huts just inside the gate. It came unhurriedly to its side of the wire fence and watched him. The dog was a young, ninety-pound Alsatian in good condition with no need to prove anything. It made no sound. It crouched a little on its haunches without any concerted effort to be threatening and watched the man on the other side of the fence. Feiffer tested the padlock on the wire. The dog made a deep growling noise and went down a little lower on its spring loaded thigh muscles. Feiffer stepped back from the gate. He went back to his car, unlocked it, and pressed the horn button three times. Behind the wire, the dog sat and watched him.

A man's voice from somewhere to one side of his car asked Feiffer out of the darkness in English, 'Yes?' The dog got up and began making low snarling noises. There was someone in the shadows, coming towards him: a tall man wearing a cap. He came closer: he was in uniform. He asked again, 'Yes?'

'Who are you?'

The tall man in the uniform (it had a flash on the shoulder with the word SECURITY embroidered on it in gold letters) ignored the question. He had a truncheon on his belt and something slung over his shoulder. Like the dog, he made no effort to be frightening. The thing slung over his shoulder was a shoulder-stocked Mauser broomhandle automatic pistol. The man asked in accented English, 'Who are you?' He asked, 'Are you lost?'

Feiffer said, 'I'm a police officer. Who are you?'

The security guard (now that he was closer Feiffer could see he was prematurely bald under the cap) said, 'May I see your identification?' He had an unhurried, even sort of voice with an accent that sounded Portuguese. He said reasonably, 'You'll appreciate my request.'

Feiffer took out his warrant card and opened it. The security guard shone a flashlight into it and looked hard at the photograph. He said in that same, calm tone, 'What can I do for you, Chief Inspector?' He said to the dog in an easy conversational tone, 'Friend.'

'You are—?'

The security guard said, 'Mr Mendoza.' He moved forward to the wire gate and took out a key for the padlock, 'Come inside and have a cup of coffee.' He unlocked the gate, held it open for the Chief Inspector (the dog cast a final glance at Feiffer), and then, when he had come through himself, relocked the door. (The dog came up and licked Feiffer's hand.) He said to the dog, 'Coffee,' and to Feiffer, 'He likes it. He has it out of a bowl.'

'Oh.'

Mendoza said, 'He'd have it out of a cup like me only his nose is too long.' He patted the dog man-to-man on the head and said, 'I told him you liked coffee but your nose is too long to drink out of a cup.' He said to the dog, 'Ha, ha.'

The dog made a sound that Feiffer could have sworn was 'Ho, ho.'

'Hmm,' Mendoza said, 'What can I do for you?' They went into Mendoza's hut where there was a pot of coffee percolating on a primus stove under a shelf. There was a box of ammunition on the shelf and something that looked like a disassembled battery-electric toothbrush. He asked, 'Sugar and milk?' and unslung the Mauser and propped it carefully in a corner.

'Black.' It was a toothbrush. The man must have been repairing it.

Mendoza said to the dog, 'The same as you.' He poured the dog a cupful of coffee into its bowl and then went to pour out Feiffer's and his own.

Feiffer glanced at the dog. Dogs usually made slurping noises drinking out of bowls. This one didn't. It sipped. Feiffer said pleasantly, 'I'm looking for a man named Wong. I thought there'd be a night shift working.'

Mendoza shook his head. 'New Government regulations about noise. Can't fire off any explosions after 6 p.m.' He said unnecessarily, 'The dog and I keep an eye on things until the morning shift starts at 5 a.m.' He said, 'Wong's a fairly common name.' He said, 'Funnily enough though, in all the time I've been here we've only ever had one Wong work for us.' He said by the way of explanation, 'When I get bored I read the personnel records in the office to make sure everyone's who and what they say they are.'

'This particular Wong has a brother who runs a chestnut stall on the corner of Yellowthread Street and Canton Street.'

'That's right.' The dog finished its coffee and waited for Mendoza to refill the bowl.

'You know him?'

'Which one?'

'The chestnut—'

'I knew his brother worked here.'

'What's he like?'

'The chestnut—'

'The one who works here.'

'I've seen worse. Why?'

Feiffer asked, 'And are explosives kept here on the site?'

'Sure.' Mendoza nodded at the dog, 'That's why we're here. Him and me.' He glanced at the Mauser, 'We don't really need that, but the company thinks it's necessary.' He said, 'If you've come to check the Arms Licence it's all right with me if you take it back.'

'No.'

The dog looked disappointed. He glanced at the gun and sniffed. Mendoza said, 'They keep about two hundred pounds of explosives in the magazine at any one time.' He said, 'It's locked up, but I've got the key if you're interested.'

'This man Wong, does he have access to the magazine?'

'No.'

'You don't know what sort of explosives?'

'Polar ammon gelignite and detonators.'

'New stuff?'

'It is, as a matter of fact. You can't get the old brand any more.' Mendoza said, 'The factory blew up or something. It's all a different brand now.'

'And this man Wong, he wouldn't have been able to get his hands on any of it?'

'Not the new stuff, no. He might have pinched some of the old stuff.' The dog came up to Mendoza to be patted. Mendoza patted it. The dog made a faint baby-burping sound in its throat. Mendoza said, 'Why do you ask?' He smiled at the dog and said, 'The Chinks are a funny lot. They wouldn't pinch explosives.' He said more to the dog than anyone else, 'They're all too superstitious, aren't they?'

· 'About explosives?'

Mendoza laughed. Compared to his normally pleasant voice it was a harsh grating sound. He said to the dog, 'About everything!' He said, 'If you knew a way to tap Chinese superstition for profit you could make a fortune!' He looked to the dog for agreement, 'Isn't that right?'

The dog made a growling noise and licked Mendoza's hand.

'Who checks the explosives records?'

'The police.' (Feiffer nodded.) 'And me.' Mendoza said, 'Chinks can't count. So I do it.' He said, 'They need a level-headed European to do anything important.' He said conspiratorially to Feiffer, 'You know that.'

'And has there been anything missing lately?'

Mendoza laughed. He glanced at the dog's fangs significantly. He shook his head.

'What time does Wong start work here again?'

Mendoza laughed for the third time. The dog also looked amused. 'Never!' Mendoza said, 'He was fired.'

'When?'

'About four months ago. He was late two days in a row without an excuse.'

So much for the brother theory. 'No.' Feiffer said, 'His brother told me he still worked here.'

Mendoza paused. He patted the dog pleasantly on the head. Mendoza said, 'Superstition.' He smiled at the dog, 'You see. Face. Bad joss to be fired. Too proud to admit he's been given the arse. Bad luck for the family.' He said, 'It's all super-stition and luck with the Chinks, all gods and ghosts and spirits.' He said as one round-eyed trustworthy white face to another, 'All they are is a load of shit.' He said, 'If you could find a way to tap all the shit they talk you could make a fortune.' He said happily to Feiffer, 'Have another cup of coffee.' He asked the dog, 'How about you? What do you think?'

# 6

When he got back to the Station, Feiffer's phone was ringing. It was the Commander. It sounded as if he had had a good dinner. He asked in an extremely tranquil tone of voice, 'Harry, tell me straight if you think there's anything at all in my idea about the Triads.' He said, 'I've been having a few confiden-tial words to a Superintendent I know in the anti-secret societies squad and he doesn't give it much credence.' He asked, 'How much do you give it?'

Feiffer paused. He said, 'To be honest, Neal, not very much.'

'Why not?'

'Well, for a start, the Triads usually don't bother about letter bombs. They prefer planted ones.'

The Commander said, '—working on the assumption that for all their many iniquities they don't care for blowing up people by accident – innocent people?' He asked Feiffer, 'Is that what you mean?'

Feiffer said, 'It's bad for business.'

'And the other reason? You said, "for a start" so I assume you have more than one thing against it?'

'The Triads don't make a habit of signalling their moves to the police.' He said, 'If they want a bomb to go off then it goes off. They don't give the local cops a chance to get to it first. That's my other reason.' He asked the Commander pleasantly, 'Does that accord with what the Superintendent said?'

'More or less.' The Commander prided himself that he was

never one to hang on to a good theory gone wrong simply because, at the time, it had seemed like a good theory. He said, 'I was wrong about that.' He asked, 'You're the man on the spot—' he paused momentarily, '—what are your feelings?' He said, 'I gather from that strange man Ho that you're following up a lead from Wong. How's it coming?'

'It went. I've just been around to Wong's brother's address and apart from anything else he's been in Macao for the last two weeks looking for work.'

The Commander said, 'I'm holding a news clamp on it all, of course, but I don't know how long it can last.' He said, 'Two or three hundred years ago when I was a young man with a fuzzy moustache on my face and a Major's pips on my shoulders, someone once threw a hand grenade into a Korean fox-hole I was inhabiting. I've never cared too much for bombs since then.' He paused.

Feiffer said, 'And?'

'It failed to go off.' The Commander said, 'In those days it seemed the Chinese weren't too hot at putting together things that went bang.'

Feiffer said, 'They appear to have got the hang of it now.'

'I assume you have a man at the Post Office vetting tomorrow's mail?'

'Detective Inspector Spencer.'

'Good.' The Commander said, 'The nasty thing about letter bombs is that they have an absolutely unlimited target potential.' He said, 'It's like being kicked in the groin by a total stranger in the middle of a crowded street.' He said, 'I don't suppose a motive has started to emerge yet?'

'I've got a lot of questions, the prime one being why the bomber bothers to tell us in advance about his victims, and the second asking why he puts *political* on his letters when his victims apparently have nothing to do with politics.' He said, 'But I don't have any answers. We're hoping to get one of the bombs intact.'

There was a pause. Feiffer wondered what the man was thinking about in his office in Kowloon, or remembering. He said, 'Commander?'

'Yes?'

'Is there anything else?'

There was another pause. The Commander said, 'No.' He said, 'Thanks, Harry. Goodnight.'

He hung up.


O'Yee's voice was going. He was getting terminal laryngitis. He would spend the rest of his life as a prematurely aged old man rasping out monosyllables through parched lips from a brain grown crazed and whiskery from the smarmy tones of elocuted antique dealers. He said to the fourteenth antique dealer on the list in a tone of utter weariness, 'Stuffed toucans? Got any—' he paused to draw a last shallow breath, '—any stuffed toucans for sale?'

There was a long pause.

O'Yee said feebly, 'Thank you ...'

He hung up.


In the sorting room of the Hong Bay Central Post Office, Spencer stretched his back. He yawned. There was still an enormous mountain of canvas sacks spread around the sorting tables waiting to be sorted. He found a chair and sat down by a sack marked *Beat 3 Collections, Hong Kong Postal Service* on a yellow label. Spencer turned the label over and back again. The label read *Beat 3 Collections, Hong Kong Postal Service*. Spencer wished he'd brought a paperback.

He glanced around the room. Nothing much to look at. There was another bag on the floor near his chair. He leaned forward to see what the label on that one said.

It said, *Beat 3 Collections, Hong Kong Postal Service.*

At the main sorting table, Mr Choy's fingers went *flick, flick, flick* with the letters going into the pigeonholes.

Spencer yawned again.

He felt bored—


Feiffer's phone rang. It was The Fingerprint Man. The Fingerprint Man said, 'Good evening, Chief Inspector.'

'Good evening.' (No one but O'Yee seemed to know the man's name.) Feiffer asked, 'Have you got anything for us?'

'Not much, I'm afraid.'

'Did you get any good lifts?'

'Not a one.' The Fingerprint Man said, 'From the little I learnt at school about chemistry I seem to recall that one of the constituents of most commercial explosives is nitric acid.' He said, 'So you can imagine what condition the prints were in.' He said, 'I've got a few partials, but they're not usable from a point of view of identification unless you've already got a complete set for me to match.' He said sympathetically, 'To make sabre-toothed tiger stew first catch your sabre-toothed tiger.' He said, 'I'm sorry, but I did my best.'

'I know that.'

'Is Christopher O'Yee on tonight? I wanted to invite him over to my father's farm at Sheung Shui for the weekend.'

'He's on, but he's off on something of his own. I haven't seen him all evening.'

'I'll ring his wife.' The Fingerprint Man said, 'I gather by the way, that you're about to become a father.'

'Yes.'

'How's your wife?'

Feiffer said, 'Unhappy.'

'They always get that way.'

'Do they?'

'Oh, yes.' The Fingerprint Man said, 'No doubt about it. It's perfectly normal.'

Feiffer said, 'How many children do you have yourself?'

There was a brief silence. The Fingerprint Man said, 'Oh, incidentally, I had the handwriting expert here have a quick look at one of the letters – the Leung one – to see if he could come up with anything.'

'And?'

'Nothing, I'm afraid. Just a scrawl. Standard secondary school scribble.' The Fingerprint Man said, 'I thought it was worth a try.'

'I appreciate it.' Feiffer said, 'How many children of your own do you have?'

The Fingerprint Man said, 'As a matter of fact, none.' He said, 'Um—' He seemed a little embarrassed, 'Um, it was like the handwriting man, you know ...' He sounded very embarrassed. He said, 'I was just trying to be helpful.'

Feiffer paused. He said, 'I appreciate it.'

'You do?' The Fingerprint Man said, 'I believe that trying to do good is the most important thing in life.'

'I agree.'

'You do?'

Feiffer said, 'Thanks for ringing.'

The Fingerprint Man said, 'I know an old Korean fortune teller in Khartoum Street. He reads your entire past and future from your handwriting.' He said enthusiastically, 'I'll try one of the letters on him.' He said very quickly, 'I'll be discreet of course.'

'Fine.'

'That's OK? You don't mind?'

'It all helps.'

The Fingerprint Man said, 'Great!' He said vigorously, 'I'll get right on to it! 'Bye!' He hung up.

Feiffer put the phone down. Auden asked, 'Who was that?'

'That was the Fingerprint Man.'

Auden nodded. 'Everyone calls him that.' He asked, 'What's his real name? Do you know?'

Feiffer said, 'Albert Schweitzer.'

Auden said, 'Of course it is. I knew I'd heard it somewhere.' He seemed happy he'd remembered.

Spencer watched Mr Choy's fingers go *flick*, *flick* with the letters. He said aloud, 'Prestidigitation.' That was a nice word. He said again to himself, 'Prest-i-dig-itation.'

Leger-de-main.

It was a very soft woman's voice, faint, like something very quiet and fragile. Feiffer said into his telephone, 'Hullo? Are you there?'

The soft voice said, 'Is Mr Spencer there to speak to me please?' The voice had an odd accent, not Chinese, softer, from farther away.

Feiffer said, 'I'm afraid Mr Spencer isn't here at the moment. This is Chief Inspector Feiffer speaking.'

'Harry?' the voice broke up into two syllables, testing it.

Feiffer said, 'Who is this?'

The voice said (Feiffer thought, 'If I heard a voice like this coming out of a Chinese girl in Hong Kong I'd think she'd been watching too many reruns of Suzie Wong movies'), 'I am Bill's friend, Frances Nu.' She was Burmese.

'Frances?'

'Yes.'

Feiffer tried to recall Spencer mentioning someone named—

He said suddenly, *'Frank? Are you Frank*?' He said, 'Good God!'

The soft voice said from a long way away, 'Pardon?'

'I meant I, ah—' Feiffer said, 'Of course I've heard him speak of you.' He said quickly, 'In a discreet way. I have the impression he's rather hiding you away.' He asked, 'Nu is a Burmese name, isn't it?'

'Yes. My family was originally from Rangoon.' She said happily, 'Bill Spencer is from Stratford-upon-Avon in England, did you know that?'

'Is he?'

'Yes.' Frank said, 'Where Shakespeare was born.'

'Oh, yes.'

'I'm studying English literature at the University.' She said, 'It was very fortunate for me.'

'Quite.'

Frances Nu said in her soft voice, 'He's very nice, isn't he?'

'Bill? Very.'

Frank said, 'I worry about him. He's much too nice to associate with criminals, don't you think?'

'Yes.' Feiffer said, 'We try to give him the less sordid jobs.' He asked, 'Have you known him long?'

'Not long.' Frances Nu said, 'I telephone him every day.' She asked, 'Is that allowed?' She said, 'Bill says you are the best man he has ever met so I thought you wouldn't mind.'

At that point Feiffer thought he wouldn't have minded if she rang up every day to order the execution of orphans and cripples. She had the softest voice he had ever heard. 'That's perfectly all right, of course.'

'Thank you, Chief Inspector.'

'Harry.'

'Frances.' Frances said, 'You can call me Frank if you like.'

Feiffer said, 'If that's Bill's name I'll stick to Frances.'

'Yes.' Frances said, 'I suppose you all think a lot of Bill.'

Feiffer smiled. He said, 'Yes.' He said, 'He's out at the moment, but I'll certainly tell him you rang.'

'It's not a dangerous job?' She sounded alarmed.

'No. He's just keeping an eye on something.' Feiffer said, 'The job is about as dangerous as counting cream puffs.' He thought, 'No, that's—' He said quickly, 'On the other hand, it is extremely important.' He said, 'Bill is one of the few people

I trust to bring his intelligence to bear on a problem and work from his own initiative.' He thought The Fingerprint Man would have approved of that one. He said, 'But there's no danger.'

Frances Nu said, 'I love him, you see.' She sounded vaguely as if she was crying.

There was a pause. Feiffer said, 'I'm certain it's mutual.' He thought, 'If it isn't I may just smash his face in.' He said, 'I know it is.' He said, 'I'll get him to telephone you the moment I see him.'

'Thank you.' Frances Nu said, 'I suppose you're very anxious to see whether you have a son or a daughter.' She said, 'Bill told me your wife is about to have a baby.'

'Yes.' Feiffer said, 'It's rather lucky that Bill is – from where he is if you're studying Shakespeare.'

Frances Nu said, 'Yes.' There was a pause. She said, 'It was a coincidence.' She said, 'I met Bill before I knew that.' She didn't want Feiffer to get the idea that she was a wanton Shakespearean using someone's birthright for her own evil examination-passing ends. She said, 'It was a coincidence.'

'Of course.' Feiffer said, 'I realize that. But rather a lucky turn of events.' He thought, 'Every way I say it it sounds cynical.' He said, 'That's terrific for both of you.' He thought, 'I haven't been so tongue-tied with a woman for—' He thought, 'For a long time.' He said to Frank, 'I'll certainly tell him.' He said, 'I thought I'd ring my wife to see how she is.' (He thought, 'What did I say that for?') He thought, 'Maybe I will.'

'Goodbye, Harry.'

'Yes.'

And she was gone.

Feiffer thought, 'Dammit, I will ring her!' He would. By God, he would. Why not? He'd ring – he would. He picked up the telephone and looked at it for a moment. He started dialling the number. He snarled at Auden, 'And don't you bloody-well try to say anything funny, all right?'

Auden looked up from his desk.

Feiffer warned him, 'All right?'

Auden looked dazed. He shook his head. He hadn't been going to say anything.

Auden said, 'What did I say?'

\*

Mr Choy's prestidigitatious fingers stopped. They froze. They began to tremble. They stopped.

A silence fell. Spencer stood up. 'Have you got one?'

Mr Choy shook his head. There was a ragged pile of manilla envelopes on the steel topped table in front of him. He moved them gently to one side with the palm of his hand, very lightly. Mr Choy swallowed.

Mr Choy said very quietly, 'I've got two.' He closed his eyes for a moment. Spencer came forward with the photostat of the handwriting. He looked at the photostat and then at the writing on the two separated envelopes on Mr Choy's table.

Mr Choy asked, 'Yes?' He opened his eyes.

Spencer nodded.

The writing was identical.

At the other end of the line, Nicola Feiffer picked up the telephone.

Feiffer said, 'I was feeling so good that I thought I'd—'

Nicola Feiffer said, 'You've changed your mind!'

'About what?'

'About the pet of course – about having a cat or a dog in the apartment.'

'Well, no—'

'I thought you had!'

'No!'

'Then thanks a lot for ringing!' She added, for good measure, 'You lousy, miserable, rotten two-faced swine!' And hung up.

Mr Hwang shrieked, 'No!' He stood a few feet back from the table with Spencer and Mr Choy looking at the two envelopes. He demanded from Spencer in a shocked whisper, 'Are they real?' He glanced around the sorting room at his fixtures, his machines, his life's work. He yelled, not having received an answer, not having given Spencer more than two and a quarter seconds to form one, 'Are they real? ! !'

'Calm down.' Spencer said quietly to Mr Choy, 'What made you notice them?'

Mr Hwang said, 'Who cares? Do something!'

Mr Choy said, 'They were heavy.'

Spencer nodded.

Mr Hwang said, *'Well? Well?'*

Spencer ran his hand over his tie. It was a Thai silk one, borrowed from his flatmate. It felt soft. He wiped his palm on the tie without anyone noticing.

Mr Hwang said, 'Well – *defuse them*!'

Spencer paused. One of the long envelopes was addressed to the Yellowthread Street Police Station, to Feiffer. Spencer leaned forward and moved that one aside with a pencil. He said to Mr Hwang, 'That one isn't a bomb.' He looked at the other. It was addressed to a Mr Dien in the Street of Undertakers. That one was. He said, 'It's only this one.' He said to Mr Hwang, 'I want everyone on this floor to go outside into the street and also the people on the floor above. While you're doing that I'll telephone Bomb Disposal and the Fire Service and have it taken away.' He said, 'There's no need for anyone to panic.' He had a picture of Frank in his mind. He said, 'It won't go off provided an attempt isn't made to open it.' He thought, 'I hope.' He said to Mr Hwang, 'Just don't touch it, all right?'

Mr Hwang looked at him. He glanced around the sorting room, at his part of the world, his life's responsibility. He looked doubtful. He nodded. He glanced at something out of Spencer's view behind the sorting table and nodded again. He went suddenly calm. He nodded. He said to Spencer, 'It's all right now.' He smiled. He said, 'I've seen this sort of thing on American television programmes.' He nodded yet again.

Spencer glanced at him. He nodded too. It was easy to calm people down if you stayed calm yourself. Spencer said, 'I'm just going into your office to telephone.' He waited for Mr Hwang's reaction.

Mr Hwang smiled. There was something a little odd about it. Spencer went towards the office and went in. He shut the door behind him and began dialling the numbers. He thought, 'He calmed down very quickly.' He shrugged.

An efficient military voice at the other end of the line said, '51 Infantry Brigade, Duty NCO speaking.'

Spencer said, 'Engineers, please, BD Section.'

'Suh!' There was a series of clickings. Behind him, the door opened and Mr Hwang came in looking pleased with himself.

Another military voice said, 'BD.'

Mr Hwang said, 'Everything's all right now.' He said, 'I put it in a bucket of water.'

The military voice said again, 'BD—'

Spencer said, 'What?'

'I put it in a bucket of water.' Mr Hwang said, 'Everybody knows that fixes bombs.' The fact that paper envelopes are soluble in water and that the trigger mechanism of letter bombs is only held back by that same paper envelope was neither here nor there. It hadn't occurred to him. Mr Hwang said happily, 'So you can just take it away the way they do on television.'

The voice said irritably, 'Bomb Disposal – who the hell is this?'

Spencer looked at Mr Hwang. Mr Hwang smiled. Spencer said, 'Oh, my God—'

Mr Hwang said—

Spencer slammed the phone down and ran for the bucket of water.

O'Yee thought, 'To hell with it!' He took off his glasses and put his coat on. He thought, 'Screw it, I'll ring the rest of them in the morning.' He looked at his watch. It was 8.15 p.m. He thought, 'It's too late now anyway.' He put his glasses carefully into their leather case, slipped the case into his inside coat pocket, and went home.

The envelope came out of the water dripping wet. The paper was going. A piece of a corner of the envelope came away in his fingers. He thought, 'What do I do?' There was a spring-loaded trigger in it. It had to be held down. He put the envelope on the steel table and slapped the palm of his hand down on top of it. He felt the dissolving paper stick to his hand. He pressed down on it. There was a faint click. He thought, 'It's armed itself!' He pressed hard on the envelope. Something held against the pressure and there were no more noises. He yelled to Mr Choy, 'Get me a flashlight!' He raised his hand a fraction and the spring pressure relaxed. The seam of the envelope seemed to be going: he felt it raise up with his hand. He roared at Choy, 'A flashlight!' There was another faint click. He thought, 'Calm. Nothing's happened yet.' He thought, 'Calm. Do it in some sort of order.' He thought, 'See what's inside and then—' He heard a clattering sound. Someone was

83

running. He saw Choy and Hwang running for the stairs. He thought, 'A flashlight—' There was one on the next table for checking the pigeonholes. They were going to get it – he thought, 'They've gone.' He tried to reach the flashlight with his free hand, but it was too far away. There was a metallic straining noise from inside the envelope. He pressed harder on the paper. The noise stopped.

Spencer swallowed. He thought, 'A letter bomb contains a charge of explosive, a detonator, and some sort of triggering device.' So far so good. That had been in the Home Office pamphlet. He thought, 'The effective range of a—' Better to think of something constructive. 'The arming wire usually protrudes from the envelope casing and is pulled out to set the trigger.' He could feel something sharp under his hand. It was the end of the wire. The pamphlet had said, 'X-ray photographs of the device in question are first taken so that a thorough study of the mechanism can be—' That was no bloody use. He reached in his pocket with his free hand and took out his pocket knife, got it open with his fingernail and slid it under his hand. He felt the point of the blade touch the wet paper. He got down on his knees and tried to look under the palm of his hand to see where the blade of the knife lay. It was too dark. He raised the palm of his hand a fraction. There was the creaking sound again. It was something straining against a tiny spring, like a clothes peg held back under pressure. He slid the point of the knife and contacted something metallic. He had a picture of Frank in his mind. He thought, 'I'm going to be killed.' He moved the point of the knife along through the dissolving paper under his palm and felt something soft. He pressed in with the knife. The knife penetrated as if into clay. That was the gelignite. There was a faint smell. Then the smell was gone.

Spencer thought, 'Between the charge and the spring there has to be a wire.' He thought, 'Not the arming wire: that only sets the trigger.' He thought, 'There has to be some sort of wire between the charge and the trigger.' He thought, 'There must be two wires: one from the trigger to the detonator and one to arm the thing.' He thought, 'If I set the detonator off, the charge will still go.' He thought, 'Maybe the detonator's built into the charge.' He thought, 'Of course, it must be: it has to be inserted.' He slid the point of the knife back away from the charge and touched something soft. Maybe it was the wire. He pressed it ever so slightly. Something gave. He thought, 'If I break the arming wire, it'll go off.' He tried to get a picture of the envelope under his hand. He thought, 'Is it logical that the charge should be at one end and the trigger at the other?' He thought, 'It isn't. It'd be together.' He remembered that the pamphlet had said that squares of cardboard were often packed into letter bombs to confuse their outline. He thought, 'Maybe I'm just touching the cardboard.' He moved the knife point back to the explosive and pushed on the point. The knife went in a few centimetres and then stopped. He thought, 'The detonator has to be in the body of the charge.' He moved the knife out of the charge and back, then in again. The knife went into the clay substance again. He slid it out. He felt another section of the envelope dissolve under the heat from his hand. He pushed the point of the knife in again. It pressed against something hard. He pushed on it. The hard thing moved. He withdrew the knife and moved it along another centimetre. There was no resistance at all. There was some sort of empty gap. He put the knife back in against the metallic object and twisted it around. Something came loose. He withdrew the knife and pushed it in again and twisted it. Whatever it was was definitely loose. It came totally loose. He pressed the knife against it. There was a slight resistance. He moved the knife a few millimetres and sawed it backwards and forwards. Nothing happened. He sawed at it again and again.

There was a faint click. The detonator, separated from its wire, came out from under his hand.

Spencer closed his eyes and lifted his hand up from the envelope.

There was a *CLICK*! as the trigger mechanism flew forwards and then, as it tore through the soggy paper, the seam of the envelope split.

Spencer opened his eyes. Laid out on the steel-topped table in front of him like a dissected frog on a biology table, was a letter bomb.

The detonator was still in his other hand. He put it on the table. He looked at the second letter – the one addressed to the Police – and put it and his pocket knife in his inside coat pocket. He sat down on the floor with the back of his head resting against the edge of the steel-topped table and thought he would wait for someone to come.

He tried, but he couldn't get the picture of Frank back in his mind.

He couldn't even remember what she looked like.


# 7

*Hong Kong is an island of some 30 square miles under British administration in the South China Sea facing the Kowloon and New Territories areas of continental China. Kowloon and the New Territories are also British administered, surrounded by the Communist Chinese province of Kwangtung. The climate is generally sub-tropical, with hot, humid summers and heavy rainfall. The population of Hong Kong and the surrounding areas at any one time, including tourists and visitors, is in excess of four millions. The New Territories are leased from the Chinese. The lease is due to expire in 1997, but the British nevertheless maintain a military presence along the border, although, should the Communists who supply almost all the Colony's drinking water, ever desire to terminate the lease early, they need only turn off the taps. Hong Bay is on the southern side of the island and the tourist brochures advise you not to go there after dark.*

It was 5 a.m., still dark; there was a light morning rain falling. A covey of ricksaw men toiled by the Yellowthread Street Police Station and went away down Wyang Street towards the centre of Hong Kong and the morning's influx of tourists. A stream of taxis went by in a line of yellow and black and followed the rickshaw men, caught up to them on the corner and passed them going towards the flyover and the cross-harbour tunnel. A solitary pneumatic hammer working on a small emergency road repair somewhere in the west of the district fired off a burst of compressed air like a distant machine gun and then was silent, then fired another, then stopped. The Police Station, seen from the outside, looked still and deserted. It was an old Victorian building on two floors, and in the lightening morning, it looked like a slightly run-down Welsh chapel protecting its simple and unwavering Welsh morality intact behind frosted and barred windows. Cold-engined police cars, their *POLICE* signs dew glistening and unlit, stood about in the courtyard at the rear of the building. There was a chill in the air. Another stream of taxis went by with their lights and heaters on, their diesel engines making a cosy chugging sound and then the pneumatic hammer a long way off fired a short burst and was silent. There were lights on on the two floors of the Station, but the windows were either frosted or curtained and there appeared to be no movement behind them. A uniformed Chinese Constable went across the courtyard past the cars into a garage at the back and closed the door behind him. Someone taking a dog out for an early morning walk stopped by the open iron gates and looked in. There was nothing to see. He walked on.

It was 5 a.m.

O'Yee looked into the Detectives' Room on his way to the interview room and glanced at the unopened letter on Feiffer's desk. He said happily, 'It's probably another bomb.' He thought he would go through the unclassified listings. He asked, 'Who the hell took the telephone directory from the interview room?' He saw the missing tome on Spencer's desk and said, 'Ah-ha. It was you.' He said, 'Ah-ha' and took it back. He asked Feiffer on the way out, 'Anything new on the mad bomber?'

'No. How about your job?' Feiffer asked irritably, 'Just what the hell is your job anyway?'

'Confidential.' O'Yee said to Spencer, 'I heard about what you did last night.' He said again to Feiffer, 'Confidential. Very secret.'

Auden looked at him.

O'Yee said, 'Very hush hush.' He settled the stolen directory more firmly under his arm.

Auden said, 'Special Branch!'

O'Yee looked around. 'Who is?'

Auden said, 'You are! You're doing something special for Special Branch!'

Feiffer shook his head. He began opening his letter.

O'Yee said, 'Am I?'

'Yes! You're doing something for Special Branch! It's to do with your promotion!' He said, 'Isn't it?'

O'Yee looked at Feiffer. Feiffer was trying to find a loose edge on the flap of the envelope and start it with his thumbnail. He was being careful not to smudge the brown manilla paper with fingerprints. O'Yee said to Auden, 'No.'

Spencer said, 'Are you?'

'Am I what?'

Auden said testily, 'Doing a job for Special Branch.' He glanced at Feiffer for confirmation. Feiffer ignored him. He found an edge and flicked at it delicately with his nail.

O'Yee said, 'No.'

'They always say that!'

'Who do?'

'Special Branch!'

O'Yee said, 'Oh.' He started to ask what people who weren't doing a job for Special Branch said when they weren't doing a job for Special Branch. He saw something on the seam of the letter. He shouted at Feiffer, 'For Chrissakes don't open it!'

There was a *CLICK*!

Auden said, 'What the hell—'

Spencer said, 'Oh my God—' He looked at Feiffer. Feiffer had the envelope in his hands. It had split open. It was a letter bomb. Spencer said, 'Oh my—'

There was a silence.

At the flyover that links Hong Bay to the cross harbour tunnel Constable Lee looked up to the pedestrian bridge where Constable Sun was and shrugged.

Constable Sun shrugged back. If there had been anyone on the bridge earlier throwing soft drink cans down on to the flyover then they certainly weren't around now.

Constable Lee glanced back at the flyover. The early morning traffic was building up. He thought he might catch a speeder. He waved to Constable Sun that he could hang on at the flyover for a few moments and got back into his police car.

On the pedestrian bridge, Constable Sun nodded. He thought he'd have one more look around and then go down to the flyover and take out his ire on a dangerous driver.

He began walking along the bridge, looking down at the traffic, listening to the steady roar of the traffic and the clicks his leather shoes made on the cement pavement above it.

Feiffer said, 'It was a dud.' He examined the remains of the envelope on his desk. It looked oddly incomplete. He said, 'There's no detonator or charge in it.' He indicated something that looked like a miniature steel clothes peg connected to wire and asked Spencer, 'What's this bit?'

'The trigger.' Spencer said, 'He's put the trigger device in but he hasn't wired it up to anything.' He said quietly to Feiffer, 'I had no idea that the second one was a—' He said, 'I thought it was just a letter.' He said, 'I'm sorry, Harry.' He said, 'I – I didn't know the bloody thing was a bloody bomb!' He seemed on the edge of tears. He said, 'I just didn't know it was a—' He said, 'Harry—'

Feiffer said, 'It isn't a bomb. It's a letter.' He turned the thing over with the end of his pencil and looked at the split seam along the back, 'Our little friend is still in the business of sending warnings to the cops and this is one of them.' He glanced at the postmark on the other side. It was the standard Hong Bay symbol posted anywhere in the district. He said, 'There isn't a letter in it in the usual sense.' He said to Auden, 'Which is odd, since both times before he's given us the name of the person he was going to kill.' He asked Spencer, 'Who was last night's addressed to?'

'Dien in the Street of Undertakers.'

'Well, there isn't any letter in here saying Dien.' He asked aloud, 'Why not?'

O'Yee said, 'I have to go.' He started for the door with his telephone directory. He asked, 'Has anyone spoken to Dien?'

Auden said, 'Dien is an inoffensive old man who runs a funeral business. He's about eighty years old and looks like he might be his own best customer any moment. He doesn't claim to have any enemies and he can't imagine why anyone would want to kill him.' He said, 'I got the impression when I interviewed him last night that at his age he couldn't have cared less if someone did. He's all set up for the next world, not this one.'

Feiffer asked, 'What do you mean?'

'Cemeteries and all that. He owns one.'

'Oh.' Feiffer said to O'Yee, 'Any other ideas?'

O'Yee shook his head. He said quietly to Feiffer, 'Only that you're lucky to be alive.' He said, 'I have to go.' He took his telephone directory and was gone.

There was a pause. Feiffer looked at the letter. Spencer said, 'Harry—'

'Yeah?'

'Look, um, I—'

Feiffer said, 'That's OK.'

Spencer said, 'I'm really sorry. I just didn't think. After I'd done the first one I—'

Feiffer nodded. He said imperturbably to the room in general, 'It is a fact that most criminal acts are motivated by an outside physical motive: money, sex, or whatever – or that they are the work of a raving lunatic motivated by an unknown non-physical motive – by some psychological quirk.' He said, 'OK. Let us assume then, for starters, that our man is relatively normal. Further, let us assume that he is using the letters he sends us for their basic accepted use – that is, communication. Let us further assume that, since he has previously been letting us know that a letter bomb has been delivered in the same post that he assumes we may have a fair chance of stopping its being delivered.' He said to Spencer, 'As indeed, last night, you did stop it. Therefore, it follows that whether or not the bombs go off is a matter of absolutely no interest to him.' He said, 'Except in Dien's case where the police were not told. And in the case of the one I receive – the one he sends to me personally – which is specifically designed *not* to go off. He needs the cops to know he's sending bombs. He sends us one to prove it.' He said, 'He wants something and he's not worried whether the police know about it or not. In fact, he wants them to know.' He asked Spencer and Auden and the room, 'So, why? Just what is it that he's got in mind that it needs at least four letter bombs, three of them live, to convince us of?' He asked Spencer, 'Surely not just that he can make the damn things?'

Auden said, 'If that's all he's trying to do, then you can tell him he's bloody convinced *me*.' He said, 'If Dien is the only one he was aiming at then he must have the wrong man.'

Spencer asked, 'Is Dien rich?'

Auden nodded, 'I should have thought so.' He said, 'He doesn't look it, but he's probably a founder member of the

Bank of Switzerland and the Hong Kong and Shanghai Bank combined.' He said, 'You know how much people spend on funerals in this part of the world.' He said, 'But if it's some sort of extortion why blow up the man with all the money?'

Spencer said, 'As a warning.'

'To whom?' Auden said, 'So far there hasn't been a word about bombs in the papers at all. So why bother if the cops have got the thing clamped down so hard no one ever hears about it?' He said, 'It doesn't follow.' He said, 'He must know we're not giving out information to the newspapers because so far he's disintegrated two people and there hasn't been a word about it.' He asked Feiffer, 'What did the papers claim the second one was?'

'A gas lamp explosion.' Feiffer said, 'I think you can assume that whatever he wants doesn't necessarily rely on publicity.' He said, 'It's essentially a private affair between him, us, and whoever the ultimate victim is.' He said, 'It's a faint possibility that the lack of publicity forms part of his plans.'

Auden said, 'How do you come up with that?'

'*Political.*' Feiffer said, 'That's Special Branch straight off.'

'He might not have known that.'

'Maybe not. But he would have known that anything faintly resembling political crimes doesn't stay on the local level very long.' He said, 'I wonder if that's why I got a bomb?' He said, 'Maybe he wants it to stay with us and still have the political tab attached to it.' He asked Spencer, 'Why?'

Spencer said, 'The ordinary police have to give out information to the newspapers.'

Auden said, 'But Special Branch can have a D Notice served on them and stop them reporting.' He asked Feiffer, 'Has a D Notice been served?'

'Yes.' Feiffer said, 'But why no publicity? Why would it hurt him?'

There was no reply.

Feiffer said, 'And he must know we'd take measures to see that no more bombs went through the Post Office.' He said to Auden, 'X-ray security is being installed all over the island during the next six hours.' He said, 'But he doesn't care. So if it's all intended for the benefit of the final victim how does he propose to make sure the final victim knows about it? Who's going to tell him?'

Spencer said, 'Maybe the bomb is just for a straight killing.'

'Which one?'

'The final one?'

Auden said, 'Or maybe the first or second. Maybe it's a cover-up for Leung or Wong.'

'If he was after Wong or Leung why tell us and put it in jeopardy? As events proved, Wong wasn't even killed. And there must be a lot of easier ways to make sure you bump someone off than using letter bombs – if he's trying to kill anyone at all.' He said, 'No, he's after something else.' He returned to his original question and asked Auden, 'But how would the final victim get to know he had to either (let's say) pay up or be killed?' He asked, 'Who are people like Wong or Dien about to tell?' He said, 'No one. Not many people anyway.' He thought for a moment and said, 'No, let's discount Wong: he was one of the people we were warned about.' He asked, 'Who is *Dien* going to tell?'

Auden said, 'Looking at him, the pall-bearers at his funeral.' He said, 'No one.'

Feiffer said, 'Fingerprints picked up a set of partials on one of the devices that went off and you can bet your life they'll get a complete set from Spencer's bomb, so our man doesn't even care about that.' He said suddenly, 'He really is the coolest bastard I've ever heard of.' He said, 'He behaves as if he's really going to get away with it—!' He glanced down at the trigger device on his desk with the envelope split open at the seam and undoubtedly covered from end to end with unmatchable fingerprints. He said with sudden vehemence, 'Fuck him! What the hell does he want?'

Emily O'Yee raised herself from the whale-like torpor of her warm bed and groped for the telephone. Her fingers closed around it. She took it back with her under the blankets, fell happily back to sleep for a moment, remembered she had a connection with the outside world claiming her, and said blearily in the general direction of the mouthpiece, 'Hmmumph?'

A voice said, 'I'm sorry to bother, but, um . . .'

'Nicola?'

'Yes.'

Emily O'Yee said, 'Is everything all right? It hasn't started or anything?'

'No, no.'

'Oh.'

Nicola Feiffer said, 'It's terribly early, isn't it?' She sounded very guilty.

Emily O'Yee looked at the bedside clock. It was a little after six. She listened for her children. There was nothing. She couldn't believe it. What were they planning? They were planning something. She said, 'I was just listening for the children. I can't hear a sound.' She asked, 'Is Ferdie the Foetus giving you a hard time?'

Nicola said, 'Harry's at work and I can't sleep.' She said, 'I hope I haven't woken Christopher as well.'

'Christopher's at work.' Emily O'Yee said pleasantly, 'I was just going to get up anyway.'

There was a silence. Nicola Feiffer said, 'I feel so bloody neurotic I could throw myself out the bloody window!' She asked, 'Did you get like this with your kids?'

'The first one, yes.'

'I'm not going to have any more after the first!'

Emily O'Yee dragged herself out of bed. She caught a glimpse of herself in the wall mirror and thought she looked like something that had been dragged from the Pearl River along with the monthly crop of drowned refugees. She said optimistically, 'I'm sure Harry will come round to agreeing to some sort of pet in the apartment.' She said helpfully, 'An ant farm.' She said, 'Surely they couldn't have thought of that in the lease?' She asked, 'Could they?'

There was a Coca-Cola ring top can jammed in between the railings of the pedestrian walkover above the traffic. Constable Sun glanced at it. The Coca-Cola ring top can jammer was nowhere in sight. Constable Sun walked on. There was a tiny silver rod sticking out of the top of the can and Constable Sun thought, 'Someone's ray gun from the last invasion of Mars by Flash Gordon and his junior spacemen.' He wondered if they still put on the Flash Gordon serials at the old Empire Cinema in Jade Road. He thought, 'No, they changed the name to the Eastern Light.' He thought, 'It's got all snotty now.' For some reason, he thought, 'I wish they'd had radio controlled model aeroplanes when I was a boy.' He thought, 'What the hell made me think of that?' He thought, 'My nephew.'

He wondered whether it was the boy's birthday. It wasn't. He thought, 'That's a weird thing to think of.'

He looked back at the Coca-Cola can and the silver rod, like an aerial. He walked back to the can and bent down to look at it. He thought, 'It looks just like the bit my nephew has sticking out of the control unit of one of his model planes.' He thought, 'If it's been thrown away I might get it for him.' He glanced down and saw a second can with an aerial jammed into another section of the railing and he thought, 'This is really odd.' He bent down to pull the can from its lodging. It was pushed in tight. There was something else in the can, connected to the aerial. (He thought, 'It definitely is an aerial all right.'), and he put both hands on the can and yanked at it. The pedestrian bridge was deserted. He freed the can and stood up. It felt really heavy. He thought, 'The junior spacemen must be getting really desperate for raw materials,' as, in the corridor of a building overlooking the bridge, someone watching from a window pressed a button on a small radio set. From somewhere inside the can there was a sharp *click*!

Constable Sun thought, 'What was that?'

On the flyover Constable Lee got out of his car and looked up to the bridge. He indicated his watch significantly and jerked his head for Sun to come down.

Sun held up the Coca-Cola can that had just clicked and shrugged.


Ho's voice on the telephone sounded tired and crusty. He said irritably, 'Yeah?'

'Have you been able to run down the batch number of the explosives?'

Ho said, 'No, Harry, I haven't been able to run down the batch number of the explosives because whoever sent the bomb to Dien was thoughtless enough to use a piece of gelignite that didn't happen to have the batch number on it!' He said, 'I've been up again all night at the bloody docks and I didn't get any joy from there either!' He said, 'I'm sorry if I sound pissed off. If I wasn't so pissed off I wouldn't!' He asked, 'What about Fingerprints?'

'Nothing.'

'No prints?'

'No match.'

'Beautiful!' Humphrey Ho said, 'He's a clever little bastard this one, isn't he?' He said, 'He's too bloody intelligent for a terrorist.' He said, 'I hear you've been favoured with an epistle of your very own.'

'It was a dud.'

'I gathered that from the fact that I didn't have to dial direct to Heaven to speak to you.' He said, 'I've had one of my people run down this fellow Dien for you.'

'I thought you were the only Special Branch man around this area.'

There was a pause. Ho said, 'In any event, Dien is as pure as the driven snow. If he's a political then it must be for the Old Widows and Orphans Party. So far as I can see he's just waiting around to get his coffin off with him in it to somewhere with some good feng shui.' He said, 'He owns a cemetery, you know.'

'Yes, I know.'

Ho said, 'The old one by Soochow Street, the one that's closed down.' Ho said, 'I gather he's got one of the last places left.'

Feiffer said, 'So has Tam.'

Ho said, 'Huh.' He said, 'If that's the best motive you can come up with you're in a bad way.' He said maliciously, 'I can just see you in Court with a leper straining on one hand-cuff and a geriatric funeral director on the other.' He said, 'Still you never know, with a few good beatings in the cells ...'

Feiffer said, 'Goodbye, Humphrey.' He said, 'If you have that recurrent urge of yours to make some clichéd comment about building empires I'll hang on for a moment.'

There was a pause. Ho said, 'Thanks.' He sounded very tired. He said, 'Maybe some other time.'

The person standing at the window in the corridor a hundred and fifty feet away pressed a second button on his radio set and the railing at the other end of the bridge disintegrated in an enormous blast that threw Constable Sun, his can, two hundred pounds of rubble and twisted metal and a swathe of flying shrapnel thirty feet below on to the flyover.

The sound of the explosion came as a heavy *WHAM*! and knocked Constable Lee off his feet against the car and then dropped him to his knees.

He saw Sun lying on the roadway.

He saw—

He tried to get up.

He—

Everything was wrong. He saw someone coming. He saw a car stop and someone coming.

He saw Sun lying on the roadway.

He—

He lost consciousness before he could do anything to help.


# 8


Feiffer shouted into the phone, 'I've got two men in hospital, half a bloody bridge blown away in the middle of the morning traffic, the more than fair likelihood something worse is going to happen any tick of the clock, and you seriously expect me to say officially that it was a bloody water main bursting?!' He roared into the phone, 'Are you completely off your head?!'

There was a moment of silence. Feiffer said, 'Well?'

The Commander's voice was cool, even. The Commander said, 'Have you finished?'

'The question is hardly whether or not *I've* finished – the question is whether or not—'

The Commander said, 'I'm sorry, Harry, but that's how it is.' The Commander said, 'I have to take the bomber at his word and assume the basis of the attacks is political.' He said, 'Officially, the explosion was caused by a water main bursting.'

'Under a bridge? A water main?' Feiffer said seethingly, 'What with gas explosions in shops that don't happen to be fitted with gas, paraffin lanterns blowing up in the middle of bright daylight and water mains going off where there just aren't any water mains, people may just get the impression that the local plumbing around here is getting put together in Transylvania!'

'I can't help that.' The Commander said, 'That's the situation.' He asked, 'How are the two officers who were injured?'

'One of them's got a broken leg and the other's just knocked about.' Feiffer said, 'Fortunately, they were at the other end of the bridge and on the highway.' He lowered his voice and said reasonably, 'Look, Neal, what you don't seem to understand is that I need the assistance of the public.'

'I do understand that, Harry, and I sympathize with you.'

'I can't put a story in the newspapers saying the police are seeking the perpetrator of a water main explosion and did anyone happen to see a man with a radio transmitter? People are going to ask just what it was the transmitter *transmitted*. What am I supposed to say? That it transmitted a tone to a bloody bomb that blew up a water main, but it's the water main we're really interested in?' He said, 'Neal, for God's sake!'

There was another pause, then the Commander said, 'I don't think you've yet quite got the total picture, Harry: I don't want *anything* released to the newspapers.' The Commander said, 'It's a total news blackout; there isn't any question at all of an alternate version.' He asked, 'Is that clear?' He asked, 'What have you got on the bomb?'

'There were two bombs.' Feiffer said, 'They were both bombs, both of the cans, one at either end of the bridge. He just waited for a copper to pick one up, locked that one at safe with his little radio set and then fired off the other one.' He said, 'No doubt he was the person who reported cans being thrown over the bridge to lure someone out.' He said before the Commander could ask, 'I've checked, the call went through the main switchboard at the police number 999 and nobody recalls whether it was even a man or a woman.' He said, 'It was anonymous and, needless to say, the voice was disguised.'

'I see.'

Feiffer said, 'The intact bomb worked by an electromagnetic escapement device sold for radio controlled model aeroplanes.' He said, 'According to the first model shop I rang they said they've sold over five hundred of them in the last six months alone.' He said, 'They cost virtually nothing, so sales are cash.' He added, 'And the gelignite used was composed of four quarter-pound sections of four one-pound sticks, cut along the batch numbers, so there's nothing there either.' He said finally, 'The intact bomb was covered, as usual, in fingerprints, so he doesn't care.' He said suddenly, 'And we're helping him.'

'Pardon?'

'Helping him. I can't help feeling that he's using us to assist him do whatever it is he's got in mind to do.' Feiffer said, 'It's all just a little too pat: the letters to me and then the dud bomb, and then arranging a set-up on the bridge.' He said, 'It's all just a little too neat. He wants something from us, from the police, and so far, since we haven't had anything even vaguely resembling a demand or a complaint, I have the horrible feeling that we're giving it to him.' He said acidly, 'I mean, the news blackout.' He said, 'I'm sure he wants that. I'm sure that's what this "political" business is all about.'

The Commander said, 'To forestall publicity?'

'I'm sure of it.'

'Why? For what reason?'

Feiffer said, '*I don't know!*'

'Hmmm.'

Feiffer said, 'Well?'

There was a pause.

Feiffer said, 'He's got something planned that's best done out of the light of other people's knowledge. He's got a final victim or object in mind that he can't afford to have known about—'

'When? Now? Or at the time?'

'I don't know. Maybe both. I just don't know.'

There was another, longer, silence. The Commander sat at his desk in his office in Kowloon looking out at the harbour through his picture window. He lit a cigarette thoughtfully.

Feiffer said quietly, 'Look, Neal, I realize the position you're in, but I should remind you that a number of people who are definitely *not* political have already been bumped off. Surely that balances the fact that someone who is political *might be*?' He waited.

The Commander paused. He said slowly, 'That sort of question leads to questions about the worth of one human being against another. It's not the sort of line of philosophical inquiry I enjoy having put to me.'

Feiffer said, 'I need help from the public, from witnesses.'

'What other leads are you following at the moment?'

'None.'

'What about that man Wong? His brother?'

'Wong's brother is in Macao. I've told you. He's out of it. He hasn't been in a position to get explosives for ages.' Feiffer said, 'We've got nothing.'

'And there was no note in the bridge bomb?'

'There didn't really have to be, did there? I mean, the message was obvious enough. It says, "Look, Ma, I can make bombs." Neal, give me the chance and even if there is a political angle to it maybe I can catch him before he gets to it—'

'No.'

Feiffer said bitterly, 'So we're investigating a water main explosion—'

'You're investigating nothing! Officially, nothing has happened.'

'It's as bad as that, is it?'

The Commander said, 'Do you really want me to give you a quick run-down on the current state of Hong Kong politics?' He said, 'No, we're holding it down.'

'And that's final?'

'Unless you catch him and discover he's just a run-of-the-mill non-ideologized villain.'

Feiffer said bitterly, 'To make non-political sabre toothed tiger stew ...'

'What does that mean?'

'Nothing.'

The Commander said, 'I'm sorry, Harry, I really am.' He said, 'The simple fact of the matter, whatever I may have the leisure to believe personally, is that some people are more important than others.' He said, 'That's the official view. It has been since the beginning of the world. Anything else is just pure indulgence.' He said unconvinced, 'You must know that.'

'Yeah.'

'Well, don't you?'

Feiffer said, 'I'll give it some thought and let you know.'

The Commander said, 'Look ... um—'

Feiffer said, 'Yeah.'

He hung up.

There was a short, hushed pause (the minions holding their breath and suffocating in respectful silence?) and then Conway Kan's voice came on the line. He said quietly, 'Detective Senior Inspector O'Yee?'

O'Yee laid his pen under the directory address of the twenty-third antique dealer in Hong Kong. 'Yes.'

Conway Kan said, 'I am sorry to trouble you.' So far he had not announced who he was. (He was used to secretaries announcing him before he was put through.) 'I trust you had a restful night's sleep.'

'I did, thank you, Mr Kan, and you?'

Conway Kan said, 'I rested secure in the knowledge that a person I trusted had his protecting gaze upon my small trouble.' He said, 'I have not rung up, dear friend, in concern to oversee your inquiries or even inquire about them, but rather to re-affirm my faith in you.'

O'Yee glanced at the open telephone directory. He said, 'Nothing so far.'

'Ah.' Conway Kan said, 'I merely wished to tell you that, of course, I should quite understand should other more pressing duties overtake you.' He said, 'I refer, of course, to the recent happenings in the Hong Bay district.'

'Oh?'

'The explosions and loss of life.'

O'Yee said quickly, 'They were gas and water main explosions.'

There was a pause.

O'Yee said, 'And the one outside the Post Office was a Tilley lamp exploding.'

There was a sighing sound. (One of the minions gone red in the face from the pent-up breath and expiring on the lacquered floor.) Then Conway Kan said, 'I would understand if such matters took precedence.' He said, 'I had a nodding acquaintance with Mr Leung of the ivory shop, but I'm afraid I do not know Mr Wong.'

'The chestnut seller?'

'Hmm. The person who presumably brought the lamp to the Indian letter-writer for repair.' He said, 'I am better acquainted with Mr Tam, the late Mr Leung's partner.' He said unnecessarily, 'I know most people in business in the district.' He said, 'Poor Mr Tam contracted leprosy some years ago and was removed to Hei Ling Chau island, which, as you know, was until recently the place for those with that unfortunate illness.' He said, 'He is a man, in relation to this matter, of perfect innocence.' He said, 'I have known him for some time.'

O'Yee thought, 'Is there anything around here you don't

know?' He said, 'I gather Mr Tam no longer figures in any inquiries the police may be making.'

'May I tell him that?' Conway Kan said, 'He is an old man and a little upset that his final days may be disturbed by any suspicion of works not of merit.' He waited. He asked, 'Do I presume on you too much?' He said, 'I feel, as a Chinese, you may appreciate matters that are a little mysterious to your European colleagues.'

'I think you may tell him that he is not suspected.'

'I am grateful.' Conway Kan said, 'I am under a further obligation to you that you may call upon any time.'

'Now.' O'Yee said, 'What else do you know about the explosions?'

'You sound a trifle suspicious.'

O'Yee said, 'One of the features that recommended me to you was my desire to do my job efficiently. I am attempting, albeit in another matter, to be equally efficient now.' He asked, 'Can you tell us anything about the matter?'

'You, or "us"?'

'The police.'

There was a pause. Conway Kan said, 'Only that Mr Dien to whom the last letter bomb was addressed has told me he cannot think who would have wanted to do such a thing.' He said, 'Mr Dien and I are partners in a business enterprise.'

O'Yee thought, 'Feiffer should be taking this call.' He thought, 'Kan wouldn't talk to Feiffer.' He tried to remember the briefing before the dud letter bomb had been opened. He said, 'Mr Dien is the owner of a funeral society.'

'A cemetery.'

'Yes.'

Conway Kan said, 'He is in fact co-owner with myself.' He said, 'Mr Tam has a place reserved for when he dies.' He said, 'That is how I know him.' He said, 'It is a matter pertaining to the older Hong Kong families.' He said philosophically, 'Many of them are presently in reduced circumstances, but the family name continues.' He said, 'Apart from that, I know nothing.'

'You have no idea who might be responsible for the—'

'None at all.' Conway Kan said, 'I have heard, from indirect sources, that you are suffering an embarrassing time with the antique dealers.' He said, 'I regret that very much.'

'It's all right.'

Conway Kan said, 'Thank you, Mr O'Yee.' He said, 'If they are gas and water and lamp explosions, then, of course, they are gas and water and lamp explosions.' He said, 'However, amongst those concerned, word does get around.' He said, 'I wish your Chief Inspector success.' He said, 'Perhaps the man responsible is only a lunatic.'

'Perhaps.'

Conway Kan said, 'Thank you for making the time to speak to me.'

'Goodbye.'

There was a pause. 'Good-bye, Mr O'Yee. And thank you.'

O'Yee sighed. It was all too much for him.


Feiffer yelled at Auden, 'Will you bloody well forget about bloody Special Branch!' He yelled at Auden, 'Who the hell do you think they represent? God?'

Auden looked at O'Yee. O'Yee shook his head. O'Yee left. Auden said, 'I only thought we could ring them and see if they've come up with anything since we—'

'No! They'll ring us if they've got anything! All right?' The hammering and drilling and smashing and tearing down started again and Feiffer stuck his head out of the open window and yelled, 'Shut up!' and, utterly miraculously, it stopped. Spencer said, 'Gosh ...!'

Auden said, 'Well, as far as I can see, the only connection between the people who have had bombs aimed at them is that they've all had bombs aimed at them.' He said, 'One ivory dealer, one chestnut seller, a letter-writer (by accident), you, and two cops.'

Spencer said, 'And Dien.'

Feiffer said, 'Or you.'

'Pardon?'

'What if the Post Office letter bomb was aimed at you?' Feiffer said, 'If this fellow's so bloody brilliant he must have realized that someone would have been checking the mail at the Post Office. So why wasn't the bomb you defused aimed at you?'

Spencer said, 'Well, not necessarily me.' He asked Feiffer, 'You maybe?' He said, 'You're the one he addressed his letters to.'

'Then why send me a second letter?'

Auden said, 'He knows that senior officers don't stand around in post offices all night. He'd assume someone junior would have gone.' He glanced at Spencer significantly.

Spencer said, 'Or you. You could have gone.'

Auden shrugged. He thought he would definitely apply for Special Branch. Somewhere where he'd be appreciated. He thought, 'A Special Branch man would have checked the second letter.' He said, 'Maybe.'

Feiffer said, 'The only frail connection I can see—' He said irritably in parenthesis, 'We have to assume there is some sort of connection' '—is that Dien owns a bloody cemetery and that one of the suspects, Tam, who is no longer a suspect, plans to be buried there.' He said hopelessly, 'Is there anything we can work on from that?'

Auden the Special Branch man said, 'You must be bloody joking!'

'I'm not bloody joking at all!'

Spencer said conciliatingly, 'I don't think so, Harry. It's just a coincidence.' He said, 'After all, if a man owns a cemetery' (he corrected himself in the light of O'Yee's information) 'part-owns a cemetery, it follows that if you speak to enough people you're going to run across someone who has someone buried there or, in this case, is going to be buried there himself.' He asked politely, 'Don't you think so?'

'Yeah,' Feiffer said. 'So far, Forensic tallies the total amount of explosives he's used as four and a half pounds.' He said, 'Since the stuff usually comes in one pound sticks, he's got at least half a pound left.' He said, 'That's either one big bang in a Coca-Cola can or three or four smaller bangs in manilla envelopes.' He said unhappily, 'Assuming that's all he's got. And we can't assume that.' He said to Auden, 'Before you ask, there haven't been any reported thefts of the stuff.' He said, 'Your old mate in Special Branch checked.' He said as his telephone rang, 'And you can't ask anyone on the street if they saw anything.' He picked up the phone and said, 'What?'

A woman's voice said, 'I've got it!'

'Pardon?'

'Harry?'

'Nicola?'

Auden said, 'John? Marsha?' Spencer looked disapproving.

Nicola said, 'I've got it this time and there's not a damn thing you can say!'

Feiffer blinked.

'Are you there, Harry?'

'Yes, I'm here.'

Nicola Feiffer said triumphantly, 'An ant farm!'

'What about it?'

'I'm going to get one to keep me company!'

'Are you?'

'Yes!'

'Why?' (He thought instantly, 'Oh, no, I've done it again!')

'What do you mean, "why"?'

'I'm sorry I said that.'

'To keep me company while I sludge about in an oversized torpor of pure sludge carrying your precious brat when I should be thin and sexy and full of life and doing what I want to do! That's why!'

Feiffer glanced around the Detectives' Room. Auden and Spencer both found something to do. (Spencer started ringing Frank. Auden stared out of the open window, thinking of Auden staring out of the open window.) Feiffer said softly, 'It wasn't only my idea. We decided on it together.' He said, 'I know it's hard for you to feel so, um—' He thought, 'Get the right word' '—um, (non-productive? No. Useless? Oh my God – um ... Bovine? Maybe. Bovine? – No!), 'Um—'

'Non-productive, useless and bloody bovine!' Nicola Feiffer said, 'So I'm getting an ant farm to keep me company.' She said, 'Surely to God that doesn't come under the heading in the lease of keeping pets!'

Feiffer said, 'No.'

'No?' She sounded surprised.

Feiffer said with great trepidation, 'That comes under the heading of infestation.'

Outside, the hammering, drilling and tearing down started again and, mercifully, the noise was so intense he could hardly make out what she said back at all.


On the eastern side of Hong Bay, crossing over Great Shanghai Road from the direction of the Aberdeen Road sea-wall, there is an old disused brick drainage sewer that was built by Army engineers in the last quarter of the nineteenth century.

You can see where it passes under the pavement by the line of rusted-up gratings that begin near the end of Formasa Street, pass over Matsu Lane into Amoy Lane and then go off in the direction of the Bay. No one has ever found an alternate use for the drain (which is the last remaining tunnel in what was once a fairly substantial system to drain reclaimed land) and it is – and has been for a very long time – largely forgotten. There were probably plans of the system in a dusty cardboard cylinder in the City Engineers' Office at one time, but it is extremely likely that, like a lot of obsolete records, they were destroyed by the Japanese bombing of Hong Kong during the Second World War or used by someone for some more pressing sanitary need in the Occupation which followed.

The person in the Matsu Lane sewers, in any event, had no such plans. He knew where he was going, had paced the line of the drain out by the pavement gratings, and, carrying a largish parcel in his hand, knew where he was. He was directly under the intersection of Matsu Lane and Great Shanghai Road, moving slowly and carefully, bending his neck slightly to avoid the low brick roof, counting out his steps meticulously accurately in the water-dripping darkness.

Feiffer said wearily, 'We'll go and see Wong again in hospital and then Dien in the Street of Undertakers.' He said to Spencer, 'You take Wong,' and to Auden, 'You're Dien.'

He said, 'For what it's worth I'll go and see Tam and probably scare the life out of him again.' He glanced at Auden and Spencer and said without enthusiasm, 'Get on with it.'

He stood up and put his coat on.

The person in the sewer passed under an iron grating in Matsu Lane and ducked his head to avoid anyone seeing him as they passed over. The light from the grating showed the circular line of the roof into the next section of the tunnel and he went on, cradling his package in his hands. He disturbed something loose with his shoulder and it click-clicked on to the brick floor in a little cloud of dust: a loose chipping, and then something made a rustling sound and a faint squeaking and brushed past his ankles: a rat. Something a little behind the person made a sudden motion and then the squeaking stopped. The sound of the person's feet on the brick floor were muffled by the steady noise of traffic a long way above. The person stopped and put his palm up against the roof. It was warm from the traffic, and there was a steady vibration as taxis and cars, buses and the odd rickshaw went over and left their heat to seep down through the pavement and roadway.

The person stopped and worked out his bearings. He was at the eastern end of Matsu Lane, below the branch office of the Hong Kong and Shanghai Bank on the corner. The person thought about the strong-room somewhere above his head and smiled. The contents of the strong-room seemed very trivial. He took another six steps and calculated he was under the main entrance to the bank. He indulged himself for a few moments thinking about the looks on people's faces, then became efficient again and went on another thirty steps.

Above him was an Indian provisions shop. He put his hand up to the roof. It felt warm. He thought, 'All that curry,' and smiled at his own joke. He went on another fifteen steps and ducked past the second iron grating. Someone passed over it at the same moment: a girl in a short skirt, and he thought – there was a disapproving shove from behind and he passed forward, thinking vaguely of the images of thighs and coloured underwear. He counted off another eighteen steps and halted. This was the spot. Another rat squeaked past him and then was suddenly silent. The person held his breath for a moment and then measured out another sixteen and a half paces to the next iron grating.

He looked up. Above him, a man's black leather shoes bang-banged across the iron grating. The person moved back a little out of sight and unwrapped his parcel, folding the brown paper into a neat handkerchief-sized square and putting the paper carefully into the pocket of his windcheater. The person had a gold ring on his finger. He took that off and put it in the breast pocket of his shirt.

He wound up the rubber band escapement inside the control device on the body of the bomb, moved the activating lever to SET, pushed the number six detonator attached to the control device into the centre stick of the bundle of twelve one-pound sticks of polar ammon gelignite, then stretched up and left the entire set-up on a narrow ledge eighteen inches or so beneath the iron grating and Matsu Lane.

The person went calmly back through the drain at an appropriate speed, surfaced back into the world through another grating three hundred feet away, dusted himself off, got into his car and, leaning over into the back set, located by touch the tone-send button on the radio transmitter he had concealed there under a blanket. The tone-send button was made of moulded red plastic. It felt hard and cold.

He pressed it.

# 9

There were dead people still lying in the street. The lane had been cordoned off and the traffic diverted. A posse of ambulances shuttled back and forth from one end of the lane to the other, negotiating the rubble and the carpet of glass and masonry splinters and rubble in the centre of the roadway. Someone came walking towards one of the cordons, holding his head. He was a man with half his shirt charred. He only wore one shoe. He looked at Feiffer and O'Yee passing through the cordon and then at Auden and Spencer behind them and then he took his hand away from his head. An ambulance man caught up with him and took him back against the wall and sat him down. There were two bodies covered in rubber sheets by the sitting man. He looked at them without saying a word. At one end of the lane there was a woman and a child lying dead in a blanket of red curry powder from the Indian provisions shop. A pall of faintly acrid smoke hung over the lane. There was a huge hole in the pavement up from the Hong Kong and Shanghai Bank branch and an entire window frame without glass lying half-way into the hole by an upturned car. Feiffer saw Doctor Macarthur and another man by the upturned car. They were trying to look inside and the other man was shaking his head. There was a heavy humming in the air and the clinking of bits of glass falling from smashed frames, the soft hissing of something like gas or an overheated car radiator, and apart from that, nothing.

There was hardly any sound. The ambulances moved quietly as if on silent electric motors. No one was screaming. People looked at each other without expressions on their faces. Nobody made a sound above the hissing and the glass chinks. Matsu Lane was very quiet. Two Indians came out of what was left of the Indian provisions shop and looked at the blanket of red curry powder and the two dead people. There was brilliant sunshine in the street, coming down in almost direct arcs between the high buildings, and it made the curry look very bright. One of the Indians said something to the other one and the other one nodded. The other Indian looked up the street to the police cordons. He didn't know what to do. He went back inside his shop and came out with a broad mat and he and his friend laid it over the dead woman and the dead child.

Feiffer and O'Yee went forward to the bomb crater. The crater went down into what looked like a brick tunnel. There was a section of twisted iron grating half out of the hole, by the window frame, and it made the hole look like a solitary confinement cell on Devil's Island. There was someone down in the crater – one of the people from Forensic – and he looked up at Feiffer and O'Yee and then went back to his work scraping at the bricks with a palette knife. The man from Forensic had thick glasses on. They made his eyes look very pale and watery. The man from Forensic went on scraping. There was part of a body embedded in the mortar and bricks just by his shoulder: a face and a hand protruding from the rubble where the pavement had collapsed into the crater, but the man from Forensic kept looking away from it.

Feiffer turned around. Spencer and Auden were wandering along the line of ambulances looking in, and then down at the bodies under the rubber blankets. Spencer's hands hung down by his sides: they seemed limp. He walked across the road and looked down at the two bodies under the Indians' mat. An ambulance carrying someone dead or dying passed through the cordon at the southern end of the street and then turned its siren on. It sounded as if it was muted or came from a long way off.

Humphrey Ho was in the street. He came out from behind an ambulance and over to the crater by Feiffer. He looked down into the hole and at the Forensic man with thick glasses. He had a small black cigar in his mouth, but it was not lit. Feiffer asked quietly, 'How many?'

'Twenty-seven.'

'Injured?'

'Forty-three. Another eight of them won't make it to the hospital.' He said, 'There may be more in the buildings, but there aren't any cries for help so they're probably dead too.' He said, as a final figure, 'Thirty-five or -six.'

'Dead.'

He nodded. He said quietly to O'Yee, 'Mr O'Yee, isn't it?'

O'Yee said, 'Yes.'

'Chief Inspector Ho, Special Branch.'

O'Yee nodded and looked down the street.

Ho asked Feiffer, 'Did you get a warning?'

'No.'

'Neither did we.' He drew a breath and lit his cigar with a gold lighter. His hand was shaking slightly, 'Him again, isn't it?' He looked down the street to where the ambulance men were uncovering the bodies of the woman and her child and expelled a breath. 'No doubt about it.' He said, 'He's moved up in the world, hasn't he?'

Spencer and Auden were helping an old man into an ambulance. The old man's head was swathed in a bloody bandage. The old man kept touching at his leg and hobbling on it. Feiffer said, 'Oh, yes, it's him.' He said, 'You can smell the gelignite.' He said, 'It's him all right.'

O'Yee said, 'I'm going to help.' He went away towards an ambulance to see if there was anything he could do. Half-way across the street Doctor Macarthur looked up and noticed him. Their eyes met. Doctor Macarthur looked back down to something moving under a blanket on a stretcher.

Ho said, 'Your friend Dien's here – the one Spencer's letter bomb was addressed to.'

'Is he?'

Ho nodded. He said, 'I assumed you'd want to wait until the medical people had done what they could.' He said, 'I saw one of your Constables going through the buildings looking for people trapped.'

'Yan.'

'Yes.' Ho said, 'I once saw the results of a car bomb that went off in Singapore. It was in a lane just like this one.' He said in an odd voice, 'He really blew them up this time.' He asked Feiffer in a voice that had a strained edge to it, 'Didn't he? He really blew them up this time.'

Feiffer drew a breath. He closed his mind to the street. 'When the Forensic man's finished down there and the corpse has been dug out, I want to go through that tunnel.' He asked Ho efficiently, 'What is it? Drainage?'

'Yeah.'

'Where does it go?'

'God knows. Down to the harbour. It's not one in current use.'

Feiffer nodded. He got down on his haunches and peered into the hole. You could see where the tunnel went, but the entrance was half closed with fallen bricks and debris. 'I want the opening cleared.' He called out to Spencer, 'Flashlights, prods and cardboard boxes.' He looked across to a shop that seemed to be still intact, 'Get them from that shop over there.' He called out, 'Give them a receipt.'

Ho said, 'A what—?'

'Shut up. You get on to the Commander and tell him that the political tab just finished.'

'Oh, no.'

'You do what you're told!' He called down into the crater to the Forensic man, 'Have you got anything for me?'

Ho said, 'I've already been on to him. The tab stays.'

The Forensic man, looking up, was much younger than the glasses made him at first appear. He was a pock-marked Chinese in his early twenties, wearing a masonry dust covered grey suit. He shook his head. 'The device was planted just here. Fragments. Nothing else.' He said, 'I haven't been into the tunnel yet.'

'Clear it when you're finished. I've got equipment coming. I'll go down with my own people.' He called down to the Forensic man, 'When they're free, I'll get the ambulance men to take the body out of there.' He called down, 'I assume he's dead?'

The Forensic man didn't look at the face and the hand. He nodded. 'Yes.' He looked a little ill. Feiffer said, 'As fast as you can. We'll go in carefully in case you've missed anything so you can give it a second go when we've gone. OK?'

The Forensic man nodded.

Feiffer said to Ho, 'Where's Dien? I want to talk to him.'

Ho said, 'It only reaffirms the theory in the Commander's mind that the job *is* political.' He said, 'I agree with him.'

'Why?'

Ho shrugged. He said, 'The scale.' He was going to add something.

'Where's Dien?'

Ho said, 'He was taken away in one of the ambulances.' He said, 'If you're thinking that he was behind it all and he posted a letter bomb to himself knowing it'd be defused you can forget it.' He said, 'He didn't plant this one.' He said, 'He's got the perfect alibi.'

'What's that?'

Ho said, 'He's dead.'

Feiffer called down into the hole to the Forensic man, 'Just get on with it, will you!'

The explosion when it had come had thundered and roared back along the length of the tunnel. There was water seeping in through the moss-covered bricks on the roof and, here and there, there were dead rats rolled up into tight lifeless balls. Every six or eight feet there was a cairn of fallen brick and masonry and shards of light coming in from the sunshine in the street above. There was dust everywhere, grey and black and green, that rose and fell in convection currents in the flashlight beams like cigarette smoke in the light from a cinema projector. The tunnel was dank and silent. They stopped.

Feiffer said to the three detectives behind him, 'Drop back.' He said, 'Three or four feet apart, behind each other. I want you all to walk very carefully. If you see anything, don't disturb it.' He called back to Spencer, the last in the file, 'Have you got those cardboard boxes?'

'Yes.' Spencer put the light from his flashlight on the back of Auden's suit coat. In the darkness, the material looked grey and furry.

'If you see anything, call a halt and put one of the boxes over it to protect it. Anything he may have dropped, a footprint—' he threw the light from his flash on to the floor of the tunnel and saw that it was running with water from the roof— 'Anything at all.'

O'Yee, behind him, said, 'Right.' He found it difficult to draw a clean breath. He coughed with a fall of dust in his lungs.

*

In Matsu Lane, Constable Yan nodded. He said to Doctor Macarthur by the last ambulance, 'OK.' He said, 'You got the old woman in the first building?'

Doctor Macarthur offered Yan a cigarette from his pack. (Yan shook his head.) 'Yes. That's the last.' He looked back down the street at a ragged circle of blood that ran from inside one of the crashed cars, out of the car's wrenched open door, and onto the street and drew in deeply on the smoke. 'Tell whoever's in charge—'

Constable Yan said, 'Feiffer.'

'Is it? Tell him that it'll be a while before the autopsy reports are—' He said, 'You know what to say.' He got into the front seat of the last ambulance by the driver and said, 'OK?'

Yan nodded.

'Good.' Macarthur said to the driver, 'Right,' and the ambulance started off and went past the southern corner on its way to the Mortuary.

Yan watched it for a moment, then went towards the hole to wait. In a doorway by the Indian curry shop the young man from Forensic had taken off his thick glasses and was being blindly and violently sick behind a pile of fallen masonry.

Yan pretended not to notice.


The unfamiliar voice at the other end of the line said, 'Yellowthread Street Police Station.'

Nicola Feiffer said, 'Who's this?'

'Constable Yu, Yellowthread Street Police Station.' Constable Yu said in good English, 'Can I help you, madam?'

'Detectives' Room, please.'

Constable Yu said, 'Who's calling?'

Nicola Feiffer said, 'You're new, aren't you?'

Constable Yu said, 'I'm from North Point.' He said, 'This is North Point. We're taking calls for Yellowthread Street.' He asked again, 'Who's calling, please?'

'Where is everybody?'

Constable Yu said, 'May I have your name, please?'

'Mrs Feiffer.' She waited.

'Yes?'

Nicola said, 'Isn't there anyone there at all at Yellowthread Street?'

'How can I help you, madam?'

'You can answer my question!' She said, 'I'm sorry.' She asked, 'Where is everybody?'

Constable Yu said, 'I'm not permitted to give out that information over the phone, madam.' He said, 'I can take a message if you'd like.'

'Tell the Chief Inspector I'm going out to find something myself.'

'Which Chief Inspector, madam?'

'The *Detective* Chief Inspector!'

Constable Yu said, 'Name?'

'Feiffer!'

'No, the name of the Detective Chief Inspector, madam.'

There was a pause on the line.

Constable Yu said, 'Madam—?'

'Rats!'

Constable Yu sounded like he was writing it down. He said back over the line, 'Detective Chief Inspector R-A-T—?'

Nicola Feiffer said, 'To hell with it!'

She hung up.

A hundred feet down the tunnel, there was a click. Feiffer said to Auden without turning around, 'Put it away.'

Auden said, 'What?'

'The gun.'

Auden said, 'It was the flashlight.' He said quietly, 'I won't need a gun if I set eyes on him.' He said to O'Yee in front of him, 'It was the flashlight.'

The drain widened out where there had been falls from the roof and the walls. The falls had turned the drain into a tunnel and there was the sound of rushing water coming from somewhere to one side of it. O'Yee said, 'What was the name of the American in *The Third Man*?' He said, 'Holly something. He wrote Westerns.' He said, 'Holly something.'

Spencer said, 'Rollins?' He said helpfully, 'The sewers in that one were in Vienna.' He asked, 'Who was the one who shot Harry Lime?'

O'Yee said, 'That was him. Holly something.'

Spencer said, 'Joseph Cotton and Orson Welles. Joseph Cotton was the writer. Holly Rollins.'

O'Yee said, 'It wasn't Rollins. It was something like that, but it wasn't Rollins.'

Feiffer moved ahead past the falls back into the drain proper and shone his flashlight on the brick floor. There was a rivulet of dark water running back past him and a footprint on a mud bank in the centre. He stopped to examine the print as the rivulet broke through its sea-wall and washed it away. Part of the mud flat held for a moment and he saw claw marks where rats had been and the prints of some larger animal. The rivulet washed them away.

Auden said, 'There was a little girl outside the Indian shop with both her arms blown off.'

Feiffer shone the flash ahead and looked for more mud flats. There weren't any. Auden said, 'She was with her mother—'

O'Yee said, 'Shut up.' He asked Feiffer, 'Anything?'

'No.' Feiffer moved forward carefully, 'Watch for hand-prints on the walls.' He said, 'There was a shoeprint, but it's gone.' He said, 'And animal tracks.'

'Water rats.'

'Bigger. I only saw them for a moment.'

Spencer said, 'Foxes.' He thought, 'You don't get foxes in the middle of Hong Kong.'

Auden said, 'Foxes?'

Spencer said, 'Something else.'

Auden asked, 'Are you a fox-hunting man?'

'Are you?' Spencer sounded interested.

Auden said, 'No, I'm not.' He said, 'I used to see the rich buggers hunting foxes as they went past our little peasant's working class hovel, but I never knew anyone who actually was enough of a rich bugger to do it.' He asked in an evil voice, 'Did you ride to fox?' He asked equally evilly, 'Is that the expression?'

Spencer said, 'Ride to hounds.'

'Oh?'

Spencer said, 'Sometimes.'

Auden said, 'I didn't know you were a rich bugger.'

'Well, I'm—' Spencer said, 'My older brother's the one who—' He said quickly, 'No hand marks on my part of the wall.'

O'Yee said, 'Robinson, not Rollins – no, something like that.'

Auden asked, 'Are you rich, William, old boy?'

Feiffer said, 'Bloody water!' There was nothing. It was

luxurious to be away from the things that had happened an age ago in the lane. He said to O'Yee, 'Rosser?'

'Who?'

'Joseph Cotton in the film.' He said, 'I saw it on television a few months ago.' He said, 'No, it wasn't Rosser either.'

O'Yee said, 'What was it?' There was an evil smell coming from the other end of the tunnel as they approached the bay.

Feiffer said, 'There's a grating coming up.' He passed under it and shone his light on it to see if it had been disturbed. The rust and grime around the seal was intact. He went on. O'Yee said, 'Funny how you can't remember things like that.' He said, 'I once lay awake all night trying to remember the name of the actor who played Long John Silver in *Treasure Island*.'

Spencer said easily, 'Robert Newton.'

O'Yee sighed. He said patiently, 'Everyone knows that. I meant, the first version of *Treasure Island*.'

Auden said, 'That *was* the first version.'

'Crap! That was the second version!'

Spencer asked, 'Who did?'

'Did what?'

'Played the part of—'

O'Yee said, 'I couldn't remember.' He said, 'You just re-minded me by bringing it up.'

Spencer said, 'You brought it up.' He said, 'Anyway, I hap-pen to know it was Wallace Beery.'

'That's right!!' O'Yee said accusingly, 'You lousy bastard, you knew all the time!'

There was a second grating. The rust and grime had been disturbed. Feiffer said, 'This is it.' He stopped and shone his flash upwards. He listened. Outside, it was very quiet. He won-dered where they were. He lifted himself up to the level of the iron grating, pushed it aside easily (he saw that the rust had been removed and the whole thing covered in grease), and looked out.

Constable Yan began the long process of questioning the residents of Matsu Lane.

There was no one. Auden took his hand from his gunbutt and drew a clean breath. The area was deserted. The bomber had come out on a vacant lot. There was nothing. The vacant lot stretched towards the harbour in an unending nothingness.

Auden said, 'Where the hell are we? Mars?' He said, 'Are we still in Hong Bay?' He looked for a landmark he knew. 'What the hell's the area over there?' It was a series of artificial hillocks five hundred yards away, and the outline of what looked like a small, ruined English church with a stone bell tower. He asked again, 'Where the hell are we?' There was a small stone tablet of some sort on the ground, moss covered and faded with age. It had the remains of a series of characters written on it but they were too eroded to make out. He saw another, and then another, all in varying stages of decay. He glanced back at the English church. Everything was very still. He asked Feiffer, 'Do you know where we are?'

'Yes.'

Auden said, 'Is this a place?' He asked, 'What are all these bits of stone?' He looked at O'Yee. Feiffer said to O'Yee, 'You know where we are,' and O'Yee nodded.

Spencer said, 'Is it a cemetery?'

Feiffer nodded.

Auden said, 'How the hell did we come out in a cemetery?'

Feiffer said, 'It's the one Dien owns.' He looked at O'Yee, 'And your friend Conway Kan.' He said to Auden as a matter of historical information, 'It's what's left of one of the first Chinese cemeteries in Hong Kong.' He glanced around, 'We're in the pauper's section at the back of it. It's the one that fronts on to Great Shanghai Road. In the main section there are rows and rows of tombs.' He said significantly, 'Not far from Soochow Street where Mr Tam lives.' He said to the open grating, 'This is where he came in carrying the bomb and where he got out when he'd planted it.' He asked, 'What sort of premises are there in Matsu Lane?'

Auden shrugged. He said, 'All sorts. The Indian shop, a few rice merchants' offices, a couple of jewellers—'

Spencer said, 'A few shops: metalware, a leather goods shop, the bank on the corner—' He stopped.

Feiffer said, 'Go on.'

'That's all.'

O'Yee said, 'The main offices of the funeral societies.' He glanced around at the stone tablets and shivered.

Feiffer drew a breath.

Spencer said, 'Surely, the bank—?'

Feiffer said quietly, 'We'll go back to the Lane now.' He said, 'I want to know who Dien had gone to see there.' He said, 'I want to get out of here as quickly as possible, before we're seen.'

Auden said, 'God, he'll be a hundred miles away from here by now!'

Feiffer glanced around. He looked at O'Yee's face. 'I didn't mean him.' He said abruptly, 'Let's go.' He said to Spencer, 'Put the grating back the way it was.' He began walking towards the harbour perimeter of the Double Tranquillity Resting Place of Heavenly Peace (now closed). He quickened his pace.

He was almost certain he knew the identity of the final victim.

Nicola Feiffer thought, 'I will.' She laboured out of the front entrance of the Government apartments to find first, a taxi, second, something to keep her company in her weeks of foetal bane and wretchedness, and third, somewhere to buy said thing to keep her company in said bane.

She thought, 'Bloody leases!' and dropped the change from her purse all over the pavement.

There was the remains of a child's plastic doll still in the gutter by the Indian provisions shop. O'Yee looked away from it. He looked back. The doll had both its arms burned off and a long black mark down its cotton dress where something metal had ripped into its workings and come out the other side. He looked away. There was a woman's leather lace-up shoe by the doll. The doll's eyes were open and staring. The doll had black hair. The hair was dishevelled, wet and caked with something like ink. O'Yee took out a cigarette and glanced towards the entrance of the funeral society for Feiffer. Feiffer was still inside. He glanced at the doll. He lit the cigarette and walked to the front of one of the bombed-out stores and gazed in the cavity where the plate glass window had been. He wished he had gone with Spencer and Auden to help Yan with the residents. He thought, 'Robert Newton.' He thought, 'No, Wallace Beery.' It seemed old and grimy, something he had thought about too often. He looked at the doll and said, 'Shit!'

He thought, 'Are you a rich bugger, William? – My brother is – our poor hovel—' He said, 'Damn it all!' and looked in at the rubble of stock in the glassless window. He saw a bird-

117

cage on its side with something in it. He thought, 'Joseph Cotton, Holly something—' He thought, 'Two thousand years of death, war, pestilence, the Borgias and what do you get?' He thought, 'Switzerland, cuckoo clocks.' He thought, 'Orsen Welles.' He thought, 'Holly – something.' The storeowner came out and smiled at him and O'Yee shouted at him, 'What the hell have you got hidden away in that fucking birdcage?'

The storeowner said, 'What?'

'What the bloody hell have you got bloody secretly and bloody criminally got hidden away in that bloody birdcage?'

The storeowner said, 'Nothing ...' He was a short, wizened man. He retreated a little back into the corridor of the store.

'Don't you bloody well try and get back into your store! I want to know what you've got hidden in that bloody birdcage in your window! STAY WHERE YOU ARE!!'

The storeowner froze. He said, 'Nothing.'

'You've got a bloody bird in that birdcage!!'

The storeowner said, 'What?'

'Don't you try to bloody deny it! You've got a bird in that birdcage!'

The storeowner said, 'It's dead.'

'I know it's bloody dead!!'

The storeowner said, 'I didn't kill it!' He said, 'It's stuffed!'

O'Yee said, 'Ah-ha!!'

'It's a stuffed bird.' The storeowner said, terrified, 'It's stuffed. It's been dead for years.' He said, 'I didn't have anything to do with it.' He said, 'It's very cheap.'

'I'll bloody bet it is!'

The storeowner said—

'What sort of a bloody bird is it?' O'Yee demanded, 'Aye?'

The storeowner said, 'It's a—'

'It's a bloody Ramphastes Toco, that's what it is!'

The storeowner blinked. He said, 'Is it?'

'You know damn well it is!'

The storeowner said, 'Yes.' He said, 'I always thought it was a Palaeonis Torquatus, but if you say it's a—'

O'Yee shouted, 'It's a Ramphastes Toco!' He said, 'It's a bloody Ramphastes Toco, that's what it is!' He shrieked, 'ISN'T IT!'

'Anything you say! If you say it's a—' The storeowner said, 'It is, it is!'

'It is *what*?'

'Whatever you said it was!' The storeowner said, 'That's what it is all right!' He said, 'Have it! It's yours!'

O'Yee looked at the storeowner. He felt himself seething. He looked at the storeowner. The storeowner retreated a few inches back into the corridor. The storeowner said, 'It's very cheap ...' He forced a smile. The storeowner said, 'Um—' He glanced anxiously into the street for someone. There was no one there. The storeowner said, 'Um ...'

O'Yee said quietly, 'I am now going to tear your rotten, horrible shop into a thousand pieces.' He took a step forward and felt someone's hand on his shoulder.

The storeowner said to Feiffer, 'He was going to kill me!!' He took two steps backwards and then fled along the corridor. He appeared a moment later in the window and wrenched at the birdcage. He held it up. He said, 'See! Look! It's a—' He forgot the name. He shrieked, 'It's a white parrot with only one wing!' He shouted at Feiffer, 'He was going to murder me for a crippled parrot!' He waited, breathing in and out quickly, for Feiffer to do something.

Feiffer nodded to the storeowner. He said to O'Yee quietly, 'Come on.' He led him across the street, past the doll in the gutter, to the other side of the road. He said, 'Dien was going to see the funeral society about his partnership in the cemetery. He wasn't happy about something.' He turned O'Yee gently in the direction of one of the police cars behind the cordon. (O'Yee saw Spencer and Auden come out of one of the shops to see what the shouting had been about.) Feiffer said, 'I'm now going to have a little chat to your friend, Mr Kan.' He propelled O'Yee in the direction of the car and said, 'I want you there as well.'

Auden and Spencer came out on to the road. They stopped to watch.

Feiffer said gently, 'Christopher?'

O'Yee looked at him. He shook his head. He said very quietly, 'Harry—'

'Yes?'

O'Yee said, 'For the love of God, will you please get someone to take that doll away?' He screamed at Spencer, 'FOR CHRIST'S SAKE, TAKE THAT BLOODY DOLL!'

He put his hand to his face.

# 10

Amongst the other paintings and treasures in the entrance hall of Conway Kan's mansion on Hanford Hill there was a nineteenth-century coloured lithograph of Hong Kong showing part of Hong Bay in 1856. The part of Hong Bay was barren, rocky and inhospitable. O'Yee thought not much had changed. He turned to Feiffer with a puzzled look on his face. He said, worried, 'You don't really believe that it was all aimed at Dien?' He said, 'Who'd go to all that trouble just to knock off an undertaker?'

Feiffer glanced at the picture with interest, and then at another, an oil of Macao by George Chinnery. 'Dien was co-owner of a cemetery.'

'Whatever.' O'Yee said, 'How did the bomber know he had an appointment with the funeral society at that particular time?'

'He didn't. If he'd been after Dien he wouldn't have planted the bomb sixty feet away from the place he knew Dien would be.'

'So you're saying now that Dien wasn't the victim?' He corrected himself, 'The planned victim?'

Feiffer said, 'I don't think I ever said I thought he was. Dien was a coincidence. An accident. I didn't actually say Dien was the target of the bomb; what I said, was that the funeral society in Matsu Lane told me that Dien was not happy about continuing his co-partnership of the cemetery with Conway Kan. I didn't say that was the reason he was killed.' He said, 'In any event, there's nothing certain. I'm only working on an idea.'

O'Yee said, 'Which has something to do with Conway Kan.'

'Which has something to do with Conway Kan.' Feiffer said, 'It's odd that a Chinese millionaire has pictures of China by western artists, isn't it?' He said, 'You'd think he'd have something more traditional.' He glanced at the collection of pictures and said, 'Maybe it's for his western friends.' He looked at one of the three pictures of Macao by Charles Elliot and said, 'I gather from the funeral people that he's a very rich man indeed.' He said casually to O'Yee, 'I don't think the final victim – so called – is going to be killed at all.' He said to the picture of the Macao Praya in 1850, 'It isn't a question of killing.' He said, 'Dien was only the co-owner of the cemetery for tax reasons. Kan owns it all. Bumping off Dien wouldn't have got him anything he didn't already have.'

O'Yee said, 'You seem to have it firmly in your mind that it's Kan.'

Feiffer said, 'It is.'

'—who's been doing all the bumping off.'

Feiffer said, 'No.' He glanced along the long black lacquered floor of the corridor to where the servant had gone to inform Mr Kan they were there. Feiffer said, 'No, Kan's not the bomber.'

'Then what the hell does "it is" mean?'

Feiffer said—

The servant, an aged man with wrinkles, part-bowed from age and deference wearing noiseless slippers, came noiselessly and deferentially back down the hall. He made a slight bow and moved his hand a little behind him in an arc. Feiffer paused. The aged servant said, 'The scroll room, gentlemen,' in careful English. He beckoned them to follow down the long corridor, knocked on a heavy lacquered door, then opened it and stood aside, ushering them into Mr Kan's presence.

Conway Kan, seated in a carved chair, stood up. He had a half corona cigar in his mouth held in a short stubby ivory holder. He took it out of his mouth for a moment and then replaced it, drawing on it gently. He indicated two more lacquered chairs and sat back down in his own.

He looked very cautious and thoughtful.

Conway Kan tapped the end of the cigar into a little porcelain ashtray by his side. He looked at Feiffer in silence.

Feiffer said nothing.

Conway Kan said, 'Poor Mr Dien.' He sighed. He said, 'That was the second attempt on his life.' He said, 'If it had not been for your man, Mr Spencer, the letter bomb would have probably been successful.' Mr Kan said, 'Mr Spencer is courting a Burmese-Chinese young lady of my acquaintance, Miss Nu.' He said, 'Mr Spencer's brave action reaffirms my opinion of him.' He asked Feiffer, 'Have you met Miss Nu?'

'No.'

Conway Kan said, 'She comes from a very good family. As,

121

I believe, does Inspector Spencer.' He asked O'Yee, 'Did you know that?'

O'Yee nodded. He glanced at Feiffer.

Feiffer glanced at one of the scrolls on the wall. It took his breath away. Conway Kan nodded in agreement. Conway Kan said, 'It is a regrettable event, the death of poor Mr Dien.' He added quickly, 'And of course all the other people.' He said quietly, 'Terrible.'

Feiffer nodded. He said directly to Kan, 'All roads seem to lead to the cemetery.' He waited.

Conway Kan blinked. He looked for a moment at O'Yee. Conway Kan said, 'Hmm.' He glanced at the beauty of the scroll depicting the journey of man through life and said politely, 'Yes.'

Feiffer said, 'I meant, figuratively.'

Conway Kan looked at his cigar. He cleared his throat. 'Yes.'

Feiffer said, 'Literally.' He said slowly and clearly, 'In this instance.' He said, 'The Double Tranquillity Resting Place of Heavenly Peace.' He said, 'Your cemetery.'

Conway Kan said, 'Oh.' He had thought Feiffer had been trying to be Oriental. He said quickly, 'Not mine.'

'No?'

'Held in trust for the families of the—'

Feiffer said, 'Not Mr Dien's cemetery?'

Conway Kan shook his head. O'Yee thought he looked totally innocent.

Feiffer said, 'No?'

Conway Kan shook his head. 'Mine.' He said, 'Mr Dien was the nominal co-owner for the purpose of tax.' He said, cleared of responsibility now that the man was dead, 'And for the purpose of giving him capital and financial assistance with which to restore his fortunes.'

Feiffer said, 'In other words, you lent your name to him as collateral?'

'Yes.' Conway Kan said, 'The funeral society people told you all this.' He said quickly, 'I have no objection to your knowing.' He said, 'Dien repaid my consideration a number of times over. He was going to the funeral society to sever our connection.' He said, to explain, 'He had no further need of the backing of my name and he was therefore releasing me from its use.' He said, 'He was a man of integrity.' He looked at O'Yee and wondered what he was doing here. He said, 'I own a number of businesses.'

Feiffer said, 'I'm only interested in the cemetery.' He said, 'It seems a significant fact that the only people involved in the bombings who seem to have a common connection have it in relation to your cemetery.' He said, 'The ivory shop owner's partner, Mr Tam, plans to be buried there and spends most of his time watching it from a window—'

Mr Kan said, 'Ah, my watchman—'

'Mr Dien, who is sent a letter bomb, is the co-owner of the cemetery—'

Conway Kan nodded.

'—with the provisos you've mentioned. And the bomb in Matsu Lane just happens to kill the same Mr Dien.' He said, 'The other one, Mr Wong, the chestnut seller, I haven't had time to speak to today.'

Mr Kan raised his hands. There were a lot of Wongs in the world.

Feiffer said, 'And it just so happens that the escape route used by the bomber in Matsu Lane is a disused drain that surfaces in the backblocks of that same cemetery.' He said, 'Which presupposes that he's familiar with the place.' He asked Kan, 'Does that seem reasonably overwhelming to you?' He said, 'It does to me.'

Mr Kan paused. He glanced at O'Yee and remembered something. He asked softly, 'The, ah, other – matter—?'

O'Yee shook his head. He looked at Feiffer and shook it again.

Feiffer said to Conway Kan, 'Well?'

Conway Kan said, 'What is it that you want me to say?' Conway Kan said, 'All I know of the cemetery's recent history – that is to say, the past few weeks – is that my watcher—'

Feiffer said, 'Mr Tam at the window.'

'Just so. Mr Tam reports to me that he has seen ghosts there.' He waved his cigar deprecatingly, 'I know nothing more about it. I have an interest in a great number of properties.' He looked at Feiffer's face and explained, 'Ghosts. Spirits. A spirit rising from the graves.'

'Which one?'

Conway Kan looked confused. He asked. 'Which spirit?'

'Which grave?'

'Oh.' Conway Kan shrugged. 'A number of them.' He said, 'As you know, Tam is close to death.' He said, 'It is wishful thinking.' He said, 'People have taken a small interest in him' – he motioned to Feiffer with his other hand – 'I mean, yourself, Chief Inspector, and he is probably attempting to be helpful.' He said, 'That is the charitable view at any rate.' He glanced oddly at O'Yee, looking a little embarrassed that O'Yee was there to hear it, 'The Chinese, as you may know, are a very superstitious race. Everything is spirits and ghosts and superstitions—' (Feiffer thought, 'That's the second time I've heard someone say that in the past few days.') 'The cemetery is just the cemetery. There are the normal feelings and beliefs about the bodies and spirits of one's ancestors by the families of those who are buried there—' He said in explanation, 'That is what I meant by my owning it in trust – but as for supernatural happenings in the western sense – well—' He glanced at O'Yee and then down at his burning cigar. He ashed it in the porcelain ashtray absently. Conway Kan said, 'There is a slightly perturbing atmosphere in the room which leads me to believe, Mr Feiffer, you may suspect me of some crime, of attempting to kill people and, in the case of Mr Leung and the Indian letter-writer, of succeeding. Not to mention the bomb in Matsu Lane.' He said urbanely, 'Of course, I know my perception of that feeling is incorrect, but I should like to know.' He set his eyes on Feiffer's face and waited.

Feiffer paused. He said, 'No.'

'I am not a suspect then?'

Feiffer said, 'You are not a suspect. You are a person who may be able to assist with information.' He said, 'If you will not mind my saying so, a man of your years does not go scuttling through drains carrying bombs.' He thought that cleared that up. He said, 'And you have no access to explosives.'

Conway Kan nodded. He said, 'The one place that springs immediately to mind when it comes to having access to explosives is, of course, a quarry.' He said, 'Say, like the granite quarry at Wharf Cove.' He asked, 'Would that be true?'

Feiffer paused. He thought Kan was making just a little too much of relieved innocence. He said with a trace of irritation, 'Yes.'

Conway Kan repeated, 'The granite quarry at Wharf Cove?'

'Yes.'

Conway Kan said, 'Ah.'

'Why?'

Conway Kan said, 'Because as a matter of fact, I happen to own that as well.'

O'Yee looked at him.

The aged and deferential servant wearing slippers opened the main door of Conway Kan's mansion and looked at the man standing there. The aged and deferential servant examined him. He knew the man had no appointment. The aged and deferential servant asked, 'Yes?' and agedly and deferentially touched at the pocket of his white linen coat. In the pocket of the coat there was a ·25 calibre Webley and Scott automatic pistol, well worn and fully loaded. He asked courteously, 'Sir?'

The man at the door said, 'I don't want to come in.' He said, 'I've got a package for Mr Kan.' He said, 'I would have used the rear entrance, but I'm only doing a favour for a friend and I didn't know where it was.' He had a small brown parcel in his left hand, about the size of a paperback novel. He handed it over and said, 'It isn't urgent.'

The servant nodded. That all sounded eminently reasonable. (Things always sounded eminently reasonable before the long knives and guns came out.) The servant said, 'Thank you.'

The man said, 'I've got my car waiting.' He asked, 'Is Mr Kan in?'

The servant smiled.

'There's no hurry for you to give it to him.' He asked, 'He won't get it in the next half hour by any chance?'

The aged and deferential servant shook his head. He kept his hand in his pocket.

The man relaxed. He said airily, 'It's the kidnapping season, you have to be careful.' He glanced significantly at the coat pocket. He said, 'I'm late already,' and went back down the stone stairs to the driveway.

The servant nodded. He watched the man get into his obviously secondhand Moskvich car and drive off.

The servant closed the main door silently and put the package on a black lacquered table outside the scroll room for when Mr Kan was free.

\*

Feiffer said, 'You own it? The quarry? *You* own it?'

Conway Kan said, 'Yes.' He said, 'To be frank, the new government regulations on noise control after 6 p.m. are something of an economic hardship.' He said baitingly, 'Impossible to detonate all those explosions I have stored there.' He said provocatively, 'TNT.'

'Oh, yes?'

That one hadn't worked. Conway Kan said, 'Nitro-glycerine? Dynamite?' He made a faint smile and asked, 'What is it that I have there, Chief Inspector?' He said, 'Are there any other sorts of explosives?'

Feiffer said, 'Gelignite.'

'Yes. Gelignite.'

Feiffer said, 'Don't play with me, Mr Kan.'

Conway Kan said, 'Then don't play with me, Chief Inspector!' He said to O'Yee, 'Are you a part of this?' He seemed suddenly very annoyed.

O'Yee shook his head. He said nothing.

Conway Kan said, 'Loyalty in any event.' He paused and decided about another matter (whether or not the secret between him and O'Yee was still a secret. He decided it was.) He said, 'Mr Feiffer, you know I owned the quarry.'

'As a matter of fact, I didn't.' Feiffer said, 'In that case you knew the chestnut seller's brother.'

'As a matter of fact, no.'

Feiffer said, 'But you knew the chestnut seller.'

Conway Kan said, 'I may have seen him once or twice, but I am not acquainted with him.' He was going to say something about respective positions in society, but they changed so suddenly, he decided to leave it. He said, 'I simply was not acquainted with him.' He said, 'I knew Mr Leung at the ivory shop and, better, his partner, Mr Tam.' He said, 'As I informed your colleague, Mr O'Yee. But I have no other connection with the recent events.' He said, 'I hardly go about killing people, Mr Feiffer.' He said airily, 'Men of my advanced years do not scuttle about in sewers.'

Feiffer said, 'Drains.'

'I beg your pardon.'

Feiffer said, 'It was a water drain, not a sewer.' He said, 'No one has accused you.' He said, 'In fact, when you asked directly, I informed you just as directly that you were not under suspicion.' He said, 'I think you are upsetting yourself over nothing.' He asked suddenly, 'Why?'

Conway Kan said, 'I have a position to uphold.' He added, 'A financial position.' He said, 'My integrity and honesty are part and parcel of my wealth – if any—' He said, 'Some of the positions I hold, for example – the trustee ownership of the cemetery, do me no monetary good other than to advance my reputation as a man with whom it is safe and reliable to do business.' He said, 'I get no economic gain from the cemetery.' He said, 'Apart from one or two reserved places, it has been closed for years.' He said, 'To be blunt, the ownership devolves upon the person in the community who can afford to run it.' He said, 'Temporarily, I am that person.' He said, 'The bones of my own grandfather are buried there, as are the remains of a great number of the ancestors of people presently living in this district, as well as other places.' He said, 'Some of the descendants of those people are presently on hard times.' He said, 'All the remains in the cemetery are of people who did well – the ancestors, in some cases, of some of the people who are now living in reduced circumstances. The cemetery and their ancestors are an inspiration to them to succeed—' he added quickly, 'On the material level – and many of them will.' He said, looking at O'Yee, 'As Mr O'Yee knows, my own father was a poor man until he made his fortune in the Caribbean. But his father was very rich.' He said, 'My father owed the man who kept up the cemetery in his day a great debt.' Conway Kan said, 'So now I use my own modest fortune to keep it up.' He said, 'There is nothing sinister about the cemetery.'

Feiffer asked, 'Who are these people Tam sees moving about?'

Conway Kan said, 'I have absolutely no idea.'

'Ghosts?'

'I don't know.' Conway Kan said, 'It is only one person, or ghost, or spirit or whatever, and only Mr Tam has seen it.' He said impatiently, 'I have no notion of what you expect to find out from me about the cemetery.'

'I don't know what I expect to find out.' Feiffer said, 'How do you know Mr Tam is the only one to have seen it?'

'Because he told me!'

Feiffer said patiently, 'He told you that he had seen something. But how do you know that no one else has?'

Conway Kan stubbed his cigar in the ashtray. He sighed. He thought, 'This is too much—' 'Because the apparition has not been seen by a more reliable source.'

Feiffer thought, 'Nothing.' He said, 'I see.'

Conway Kan said, 'If a Chinese was going to enter the cemetery in order to do mischief, he would certainly not enter it at night.' He said wearily, 'Superstition – remember?' He said, 'And in the event, the bomber entered it and left it during the day, did he not?'

Feiffer said, 'He did.'

'So!'

Feiffer said, 'I'm desperate – people are being killed and I—'

Conway Kan said finally, 'In any event, Mr Tam's friend is sufficiently well endowed to deal with any trouble during the day.' He said, 'You mentioned that the drain was in the rear of the grounds—'

Feiffer said, 'Yes.'

'Then the visions have nothing to do with that. As I have said, they are at night and always in the front section of the cemetery.' He said, 'His friend has also watched at night when he is free and seen nothing.' Conway Kan thought, 'I can't take much more of this without my lawyer here.' He thought better of it. He said in a very tired voice, 'Chief Inspector, I am an old man, I am not up to this sort of thing—' He looked at O'Yee and said, 'Dear friend, you—'

Feiffer said, 'Has Mr Tam's friend been into the cemetery at night to check it?'

'Yes!'

'Where does his friend live?'

'His friend lives in the next room in the building in Soochow Street owned by me.'

'Owned by—'

Conway Kan said, 'For my employees—'

'Then his friend is employed by you?'

Conway Kan said, 'Yes!'

'Where?'

'At—'

Feiffer said, 'At the Wharf Cove quarry.'

'He keeps a watchful eye on my buildings and—'

Feiffer said, 'And, with his friend, Mr Tam, on the cemetery.' Suddenly, he knew the connection between Tam and Wong, between a leper watching a cemetery from a window in Soochow Street who was a friend of the rich and a chestnut seller in Canton Street fallen on hard times who was not. He knew where Dien came in, and the funeral society in Matsu Lane, all of it, the entire plan. He said quietly, 'And Mr Tam's friend, your employee, is not Chinese, is he? The one who listens to Mr Tam's stories about death and superstition and the importance of cemeteries.' He asked, 'Am I right?'

Conway Kan said, 'What are you getting at?' Conway Kan said, 'In fact he is—'

Feiffer said to O'Yee, 'They weren't fox prints in the drain.' He said, 'They were the paw marks of a bloody *dog*!'

Mr Kan said, 'The security guard at the quarry.' He said, 'The one who checks the explosive records.' He said, 'Mr Mendoza.'

Feiffer said, 'Yes—!'

Outside, the minute hand on the wristwatch wired up to its detonator in the brown paper parcel on the black lacquered table reached the quarter hour and made an electrical connection to a battery. An electrical impulse, liberated instantly in the conjoining of two terminals ran joyously down the lead in a millisecond and sent a charge into the copper body of a number six detonator. In that same millisecond the body of the detonator swelled, grew enormous under the pressure of expanding gases, and detonated the batch numbered one pound stick of gelignite pressed around it. The gelignite jumped with the sudden force, then exploded.

The telephone rang and rang and rang. It went on ringing and ringing. The telephone went on ringing and ringing. The telephone—

Feiffer picked himself up from the floor and coughed a sudden spasm of acrid blue smoke from the back of his throat. His eyes were streaming and there was a heavy bruised feeling down his back. He looked at O'Yee. O'Yee was bending over Conway Kan, helping him to his feet. Something made a heavy splintering sound and fell down from the wall like the residual rocks and pebbles from an avalanche. The telephone went on ringing and ringing on a side table near the far window. There was the smell of burning in the room and a wisp of white smoke from the ashes of one of the antique scrolls on the floor. The telephone went on ringing and ringing. O'Yee heard the servant's voice coming from somewhere outside in the hall, saying something, and then it stopped, and O'Yee was aware of something like soot or hot ash on his face. The telephone kept ringing unbrokenly. O'Yee wiped the ash or whatever it was away from his face and helped Conway Kan towards one of the chairs that remained upright. The telephone went on—

Feiffer rubbed at his eyes. Things were wet and blurred. He picked up what he thought was the right part of the telephone and said, 'Yes?'

A voice on the other end of the line said, 'This is Mendoza.' Mendoza said, 'You may inform Mr Kan that I have planted charges of gelignite all over his precious cemetery.' He said, 'Some of them in the tombs and coffins themselves, and unless my price is met I intend to detonate them.' He said, 'You can tell Mr Kan that I have made it my business to see that there has been no publicity about past events—' He said, '—which were intended to suggest to Mr Kan that my threat is not an idle one, as well as to instruct those concerned with the cemetery in the same lesson – and, it would be easier and more businesslike to see that there is no publicity about this.' He said, 'The price is six million Hong Kong dollars.' He said, 'Before you ring the police, I shall do it for you.' He asked, as an afterthought, 'Who am I speaking to?' He asked curiously, 'Mr Feiffer?'

'Yes.'

Mendoza said, 'Ah.' That was an unexpected bonus. He said, 'That saves me the trouble.' He said, 'Kindly inform Mr Kan that what I want from him, as trustee and guardian of Chink superstition, is the money.'

Feiffer said, 'You must be—'

Mendoza said, 'Ah.' He paused. He said evenly, 'And for your own part, what I want from you—' He said, 'The police, Mr Feiffer, as the guardians of the law and order that preserve the trustees and guardians of Chink superstition, is even simpler—'

Feiffer did not reply.

Mendoza said, 'Ah ...' He sounded a little disappointed that Feiffer had not asked. He said, 'I am at the cemetery now.' He said, 'Nearby at any rate. At any rate, I shall be at the cemetery by the time you are at the cemetery.' He said, '—what I want from you, from the police, is immunity.' He said, 'Total immunity from prosecution.' He said, 'And the money.' He said, 'Absolutely and total immunity from prosecution for anything. And the money.' He asked pleasantly, 'Have you got that?'

Feiffer did not reply. He looked dazedly around the shattered room.

Mendoza said, 'All right?'

'I understand what you're saying.'

Mendoza said pleasantly, 'Good.' He said suddenly in a sharp tone, 'Arrange it!'

He made a harsh grating sound in the back of his throat and then he was gone.

# 11

The nineteenth-century stone church rotting away in the centre of the Double Tranquillity Resting Place of Heavenly Peace had been envisaged by an American Catholic as the new (and only) Saint Jude's Catholic Church of Hong Kong. The government who immediately agreed to raise the money for the idea were very pleased. They employed trustworthy Chinese workmen who had been deheathenized by the South China Presbyterian Missionaries to build it for him.

The Chinese built him a perfect replica of the South China Presbyterian Mission church in which they had all been deheathenized. The government apologized profusely to the American Catholic and proceeded to offer it to the South China Presbyterians at a high ground rent as a base from which to continue their good works.

The South China Presbyterians took one look at the church and decided they were doing well enough already and declined it.

The government looked around for someone else. Some Mormons on their way through to Zion found the Chinese very receptive to their doctrine of plural marriage and asked the government if, possibly, they might rent it? The government said, 'Certainly.' The Chinese, plurally married and content, flocked to the church to hear more. More was that Zion was located a few thousand miles away in Missouri. The Chinese flocked out.

The government said it had no idea that was what the Mormons had had in mind.

A Welsh Methodist happened to be passing. The government thought that sounded safer. The Chinese decided that if you weren't too keen to make a pious pilgrimage to Missouri where you might enjoy the favours of female multitudes, then a worshipful wander to Wales where there was nothing but Welsh coal mines and climate sounded even less attractive.

The Welsh Methodist went back to his chapel in Merthyr Tydfil.

The government briefly – in 1859 – paused. They looked around. Short of the odd Hedonist, Holy Roller and Hellfire Hollerer, that seemed to be the lot. They wondered who might just possibly have a use for a fine, well-built little section of China.

Lacking anyone better, they gave it to the Chinese. The Chinese asked what the hell they were supposed to do with it. The government suggested warily that since the land was located near the sea and on high ground, might it not just conceivably have good feng shui for something? The Chinese, who had had a feng shui diviner in three years before even the first brick had been laid, said maybe. They said, as a favour they'd take it rent-free as a cemetery.

The government said just so long as you don't use the consecrated Catholic-Presbyterian-Mormon-Methodist church for it.

The Chinese said fine. They promised never to use it for anything.

The government said, 'Good.'

It gave them a warm feeling to know they had built something worthwhile.


The Commander said, 'We're going to give it to him, Harry.' He and Feiffer stood by the open door of Feiffer's car to one side of the main gate of the cemetery. There were six other police cars blocking the gate. Another two vehicles – one from

132

the Emergency Unit – pulled up. The Commander said, 'I've talked to him and we're going to give it to him.' He glanced across to the ruined church in which Mendoza waited with his transmitter, 'The decision's made. There's no alternative.' A ray of light reflected off the silver braid on the Commander's uniform cap and made it glisten, 'You'd agree with me, Harry?'

Feiffer said, 'You're certain he's actually set up the hardware? The bombs?'

The Commander looked surprised. 'I got here as soon as you rang. I've spoken to him and I take the threat seriously.' He said, 'It's up to me, you know – to make the decision.'

'Yes.' Auden and Spencer were at the open doors of the Emergency Unit van. The street facing the cemetery was cordoned off. There were scope mounted Armalite rifles being handed out.

The Commander said, 'His story is that he's got eighteen bombs planted in and around the cemetery and in the mausoleums.' He added, 'He claims to have two or three actually set inside coffins. I believe him. He wants the money and immunity. I gather that Mr Kan's off getting it together at this moment.' (Feiffer nodded.) 'And as far as immunity goes, I'm going to see the Attorney-General as soon as I leave here.' He said, 'Mendoza's given me three hours to arrange it. In the circumstances, that's probably more than generous.' The Commander said, 'I even find myself having a sneaking admiration for the man's ability.'

'The families of the people who were killed and maimed in Matsu Lane will find that a great comfort.'

'I mean, in relation to his efficiency—' The Commander said, 'Look, Harry, I don't have to be filled with righteous indignation. I'm too old a dog for that. All I have to do is see that things keep running properly.'

Feiffer said, 'Hmm.'

'—this man poses a threat and I have to find a way to resolve it. If it was a public matter it would be different.' The Commander said, 'Thanks to the news clamp that you opposed, no one, thank God, knows anything about it except the interested parties. That means things can be resolved outside of the public gaze.' He said, 'The accurate situation is that he's got us firmly by the short hairs and the only way to extricate ourselves is to give in. So, as a relatively reasonable man, I'm giving in. It's the appropriate reaction.' He asked, 'Can you even begin to imagine the propaganda the Communists would get out of it if the British Hong Kong Imperialist war-mongering etceteras let a Chinese cemetery get blown to bits? It doesn't even bear thinking about. It's a political matter and it requires a political response.' He said definitively, 'That man Mendoza is bloody brilliant and he's going to get exactly what he wants because we don't have any choice. —Clear?'

Auden and Spencer went past O'Yee at the stone wall of the cemetery and took up sniping cover with their Armalites.

'Well?'

'It's clear.'

'I'm glad.' The Commander said, 'Thus far you haven't felt able to agree with my methods in dealing with this case and thus far, I've taken your views seriously. Now it's different.' He dropped his voice, 'I have good reason to believe that both the Attorney-General and the Governor will consent to the immunity without hesitation.'

'What about the money?'

'What about it?'

'What happens to that? Does he get that as well?'

'That's between him and Conway Kan.'

'In that case, he gets the money as well.'

'That's between him and Conway Kan.' The Commander said, 'If Mr Kan wants to make a gift of money to someone that's his own affair. It doesn't concern the police.'

There was a silence. The Commander looked away.

The Commander said, 'In any event, that's the situation.' We can't afford the trouble the loss of the cemetery would cause.' He said, 'It's one of the oldest cemeteries on the island. There can't be less than three thousand families represented in it. Some of them still quite influential.' The Commander said, 'It's a political gesture activated by—'

'It's just common bloody extortion!'

'As far as you're concerned, it's a political case and it doesn't concern you any further!' He said, before Feiffer could say anything else, 'So just leave it. Your job as the local man on the spot is to take charge in my absence and keep the area clear of bystanders, all right? Just keep the area clear and everyone in check. Have you got that?'

'What about the snipers? Whose idea were they?'

'They were my idea. They're strictly for the sake of appearance. Ammunition hasn't been issued – and it isn't going to be. All right?' The Commander said, 'Just keep everyone happy until I get back from seeing the Attorney-General.' The Commander waved at his driver to bring his car forward. He looked at Feiffer interrogatively, 'All right?'

'Is it OK if I at least talk to him?'

'To who?'

'To bloody Mendoza of course!'

'No.'

'Why not?'

'Because he's too—'

Feiffer said angrily, 'Listen, if he's so goddamned brilliant then a few words from me – from the local moron directing bloody traffic – won't make any bloody difference, will it?' He said, 'You might just faintly recall I've been chasing the bugger for quite some time now! I think I at least deserve the right to see him face to face before he flies off with his bloody money to join John Paul Getty on his yacht!' He asked the Commander bitterly, 'You'd agree, Neal? Or wouldn't you?' He said vehemently, 'You never bloody know, do you? I might even be able to talk him out of it!' He added, 'Or shoot his bloody bomb finger off.'

The Commander paused. He looked at Feiffer's face for a moment. The Commander said quietly, 'I'd be against that, Harry: anything that might jeopardize negotiations, unless it was totally successful.' He asked, 'Just how good a shot are you?'

'I wasn't serious, as well you know!' He glanced at the Commander and realized that the Commander had been serious. Feiffer said, 'My God, you people must be really desperate—'

The Commander said nothing.

Feiffer said, 'I just want to talk to him.' He glanced across to where O'Yee was standing in the street and gazing out at the silent church. He said, 'Not an army, just me. Talk. Not shoot. All right?' He waited. He thought, 'This has all been done the wrong way from the start.' He thought, 'Nothing'll change. He'll say no and it'll all go on continuing in totally the wrong way.' He waited for the Commander to decide.

The Commander looked at him.

'Talk to him?'

The Commander looked at him. The Commander's car pulled up behind him.

'Well?'

The Commander said, 'Do it,' and the driver got out to hold open the rear door. The Commander said, 'But don't be wrong.' He went to get into the car. 'I'll be back in approximately two hours. You've got until then.' The driver closed the door after him and got back into the front seat.

'To do what?' Feiffer waited for the Commander to roll down the rear window.

The Commander paused. He gave a sharp command to his driver and the car sped away.

It was 3 p.m. in the afternoon on a wonderfully bright Spring day.

... At the cemetery.

Feiffer said, 'We've got two hours.'

'To do what?' O'Yee looked out at the church. A tall figure half-silhouetted behind part of the fallen tower wall moved a few feet to one side and then disappeared. O'Yee had a strange look on his face. He looked at Feiffer and then across to the main entrance of the cemetery where the uniformed men were, 'From what I hear he's got the game sewn up.' O'Yee said, 'I've been watching the uniformed men – the Chinese. They're not happy about this.' He said with the strange look still on his face, 'Neither am I. Maybe we'd best just give him the money.'

'Are you serious?'

O'Yee did not reply. After a moment he said, 'I've got a funny feeling in the pit of my stomach, Harry, like someone's just died.' He said, 'I don't expect you to understand it.'

'I understand that that murdering bastard out there has killed people!'

O'Yee nodded. O'Yee said, 'The thought that he could destroy all – it makes me feel—' He said suddenly, 'Just give him the money and be done with it!'

'And what about the people he's killed?'

'I'm sorry about that, but there's just nothing to be done! If Kan's willing to pay him, then let him pay him!' O'Yee said, 'Anything! Just so long as he gets out of here!'

Feiffer said, 'Listen, I've got two hours. There must be something – something he's missed – some leeway – can't you see that?'

'I can see that he's—'

'He's been leading everyone along from the word go! He writes *political* on his letters, so by God, the crimes are political; he sends the cops a bomb so they'll take him seriously, and what do they do? They take him seriously— He kindly leaves duplicate bombs around so we can see just how they're done and think he's clever, so hey presto he's a fucking genius! He leaves fingerprints all over the place so we'll know it's him when he comes to blow up the cemetery, so we say, "It's got to be him." He's done everything with one sole aim in mind: to give us to understand that he's in control, that he's the local bloody Fu Manchu, too clever to be caught, so when it comes time to catch him we say, 'No, he can't be caught – we'll give him immunity!' It's all a brilliant piece of nerve and camouflage. But he's made a mistake! Somewhere along the line he's done something which can't be justified! He's made one assumption that doesn't rest on any evidence or reality and that's where we can get in and knock his bloody chessboard right off the bloody table!' He demanded malevolently, 'Now where is it?'

'I just don't want anyone charging about setting him off!' O'Yee said, 'Why not just let Kan pay him the money?'

'Because that's not the way things are supposed to be done! This is not going to happen behind closed doors! Even the bloody rifles aren't loaded— Now, I want your assessment of the situation so far!'

'My assessment of the situation is that it's all over!'

'It isn't all over by a long shot. It's just starting. The investigation is just starting. So far, he's called every one of the shots and while we thought we were investigating a series of bombings all we were really doing was helping him: being his errand boys. Well, that's over. So now we go back to square one. So we start our investigation *now*.'

O'Yee said, 'Why the hell do you think the only people with the rifles are Auden and Spencer? Because there isn't a Chinese copper in the whole of Asia who'd start shooting in a place like this!' He said, 'If they didn't know that ammunition hasn't been issued, they'd tear Auden and Spencer to pieces!'

'What about Mendoza? Why don't they tear *him* to pieces?'

'Because he's got the graves of their families and the families of their friends wired up with goddamned gelignite, that's why! You get rid of that and Mendoza won't even make it to the nearest police car!' He said definitively, 'But he has got the gelignite and no one is going to do anything.' He said, 'I'm sorry!' He demanded, 'What the hell have we got left to investigate anyway?'

Feiffer said, 'Him!'

'Big deal!' There was a strange sound rising from somewhere behind him. O'Yee looked around. It was the Chinese Constables. They were together by the main entrance. It was a humming sound, deep, single toned, like a dirge. You couldn't see who was actually making the sound, but it was there. One of them looked at O'Yee and then at Feiffer. He looked back to O'Yee again. The sound went on and on. The Chinese Constables looked wan and drained as if their strength had gone. Their arms seemed to hang down, ragdoll-like: O'Yee knew he was imagining it. The sound went on and on. O'Yee glanced across at Mendoza's outline at the break in the wall. He thought, 'Oh my God, what would my father say?'

He said to Feiffer with an effort, 'What do you want me to do?'

Auden patted his rifle. It was an AR-18 manufactured under licence from Colt by the Howa Company of Japan, one of the few exported, and Auden was very fond of it. He had spent an entire afternoon with it on the range at the last qualifying shoot and he thought he was very good with it. He patted it again and looked at Spencer's weapon. It was an AR-16, a carbine. Auden smiled at it condescendingly. The rear doors of the Emergency Unit's van were still closed. Inside, was the ammunition. Auden drew a bead through the telescopic sights on the figure moving about behind the ruined wall of the stone bell tower and held his breath.

He said quietly, '—Bang!'

O'Yee said, 'We know why he picked those people. He picked Wong because he knew his brother and he probably wanted to meet whoever was investigating the bombings. The fact that

Wong's brother used to work at the quarry would have brought someone down.'

Feiffer nodded.

'—and Leung because he'd heard about him from Tam. And Tam told him about the cemetery and presumably about Conway Ken. Dien because he was co-owner in the cemetery, Matsu Lane because that was the headquarters of the funeral society that administered it. Us because he wanted immunity to be arranged. And that's all. The bridge blowing up was to convince us that he could make radio controlled bombs like the one he's got now—'

'Right.'

O'Yee said, 'I know it's right. Where does it get us?'

'What else did he do?'

'Nothing – he wrote us letters.'

'Saying what?'

'Saying that he was going to kill people – he was going to send bombs to them.'

'Right. And what else?'

'And that he was going to do it for political reasons.'

'Which was wrong.'

O'Yee said irritably, 'Right. Which was wrong. So what?'

'Then why do it? The one thing that everyone seems to have firmly fixed in their minds is that this bugger just doesn't make mistakes. So why say political when it wasn't?'

'How should I know! To keep it quiet? To—?'

Feiffer said thoughtfully, 'To keep it quiet.'

'I don't think I'd like it broadcast too loudly that I was in the process of blowing people up either!'

'But you don't blow people up.'

'—the point of which being?'

'The point of which being that he does.'

'—I don't follow.'

'No.'

O'Yee said, 'So tell me.'

Feiffer said, 'Hmm.' He asked the cemetery entrance thoughtfully, 'So just how did he expect to get away with it? – by being granted immunity.' He turned back to O'Yee, 'Correct?'

'Correct.'

'In that case it wouldn't matter who knew. So why try to

keep it quiet?' He asked slowly, 'Or would it make it impossible for the police to recommend immunity if too many people knew about it?'

'You'll have to ask the Commander about that one—'

'I have asked the Commander. The Commander, not in so many words, gives me to understand that it'd be difficult but not necessarily impossible—'

'How the hell's Mendoza supposed to know that?'

'Bloody Mendoza knows everything, doesn't he?' He asked forcefully, 'Explain to me why it is that Mendoza's wandering about in that church in virtually full view when he knows there are people out here with guns? Tell me, why is that?'

'He knows they're not going to shoot—'

'Oh? Why aren't they going to shoot?'

O'Yee said, 'Well – well, because of the – of the bombs and – and the radio transmitter and—'

'More than that. For what reason of law or policy?'

'I don't know – because it isn't – because it isn't appropriate to the crime in progress – I don't know. What are you getting at?'

'Why is it that he's gone to endless trouble to make certain we can see him clearly? He's now walked backwards and forwards past that hole in the tower wall, since I've been counting, five times. He's showing himself. He doesn't expect to be shot. Now, why not?'

O'Yee said, 'Do we know if he's armed?'

Feiffer said, 'According to the regulations, the police are only justified in opening fire when life is endangered.' He said, 'The dead don't come under that heading.' Feiffer said, 'So, this time, he's only threatening to blow up the dead – a few bones.' He said in an odd voice, 'Yet surely he'd achieve the same object if he threatened someone living – if he had someone alive as a hostage – surely he could get the same immunity if the person was important enough? – even if he or she wasn't. Or if he had a *group* of people threatened.' He asked O'Yee, 'Do you see what I'm getting at?'

O'Yee said tersely, 'Go on.' He glanced out at the church and felt a wave of deep hatred pass through him, 'Go on.'

Feiffer said, 'But he's chosen the dead on purpose. He's chosen them because he knows we won't shoot him out of hand because it isn't appropriate.' He said, 'The fact that he's killed people in the past – or is *alleged* to have killed people in the past – isn't pertinent to the crime in progress now.' He asked again, 'So why *political* at the bottom of those letters?'

O'Yee said, 'To keep it quiet from the people who have relatives buried here. To keep the immunity and the money strictly between the people who are frightened about what people will think about them if they don't pay – Kan and the funeral society and the rest of them – and the police; the police being the people who are concerned to see that the victims of criminals don't kill the criminals—'

Feiffer said, 'You mentioned that if the Chinese coppers here thought those rifles were loaded they'd kill Auden and Spencer – yes?'

O'Yee nodded.

Feiffer said, 'If the relatives of the – what, three? three and a half – thousand people buried here knew about Mendoza and his bombs what would *they* do?'

O'Yee said, 'They'd kill him.'

Feiffer said carefully, 'The whole point about immunity is that it doesn't actually deny that a crime has been *committed*, only that a particular *person* who committed it is going to be held responsible for it in a court of law.' He said, 'A particular *person* ...' He said, 'I wonder ...' He said to O'Yee in an odd voice, 'He's used us, hasn't he? I mean, the police. He's *used* us. Hasn't he?'

'Yes ...'

'But he has, hasn't he? Used us? I mean, completely! We've been his obedient little helpers all the way along the line – everything he wanted. We've *helped* him. We have, haven't we? Even now – especially now. That's true, isn't it?'

O'Yee said, 'What are you getting at?'

Feiffer did not reply.

O'Yee said, 'All right, so he's a coward. He's terrified of—' He said, 'But we can't open fire on him – he's absolutely right!' He glanced at Feiffer's face, 'Isn't he?'

Feiffer paused. There was a faint smile on his face.

'We can't—'

Feiffer said, 'I've got a riddle for you. Listen. What do you get if you take a Chinese cemetery loaded with bombs, a Portuguese bomber with a hand-held transmitter who doesn't believe in God or superstition—' (He said in parenthesis, 'If he doesn't have any belief in other people's religion it's a fair bet he doesn't have any of his own.') '—a Detective Chief Inspector with a reasonably devious mind who's been left temporarily in charge, a series of letters with one word wrong in them each time and, finally, a Special Branch man who smokes cigars?' He asked, 'Well? Tell me. What do you get?'

'What are you talking about?'

'What you get, if the Portuguese bomber who doesn't believe in God or superstition isn't very careful indeed, is one arrested Portuguese bomber!' He said, satisfied, 'So let's get on with it, shall we?' He went towards the nearest police car and reached inside for the radiotelephone. He said aloud to himself, 'First, the Special Branch man—' He pressed the transmit button on the radio and asked to be patched through to Humphrey Ho. He said into the microphone, 'Urgent.' He glanced back at O'Yee still standing by the main entrance and called back, 'And for God's sake, don't say, "I hope you know what you're doing!"'

O'Yee shook his head.

A voice at the other end of the radio connection said, 'Hotel Baker One, this is Sierra Baker One, Chief Inspector Ho—'

The enthusiastic look had gone from Feiffer's face. It had been replaced by something harder. He said decisively into the radio, 'Ho? Harry Feiffer. I want a favour.'

O'Yee glanced across the cemetery towards the ruined church. He looked at his watch. It was 3.30 p.m.

O'Yee tried to light a cigarette. He had a strange feeling at the back of his neck and spine, like a tingling. It made his hands shake.

Humphrey Ho said incredulously, 'Ye Gods, Harry, you can't possibly be serious—!!'

# 12

O'Yee said, aghast, 'A *what*? Ho's laying on a *what*?' He said, 'Do you mean to say you got in touch with Ho and ordered him to—' He said unbelievingly, 'Do you mean a full scale *riot*?'

Feiffer said, 'Hmm.' He looked pleased with himself.

O'Yee said, 'You must be crazy! What's a *riot* supposed to do?'

'It's supposed to stop Mendoza.'

'—a riot!' O'Yee said suddenly, 'They won't come.' He shook his head. 'They won't come.' He thought of the beach at Hop Pei Cove. 'No.' He said to Feiffer a little less loudly, 'They won't come.' He sounded relieved, 'No. Thank God. That'd be the end of you, Harry – if they did. The Commander'd have your balls for breakfast!'

Feiffer said, 'Don't worry about it.' He began walking un-hurriedly in the direction of the cemetery entrance.

'Where are you going?' O'Yee said, 'Listen! They won't come! Forget it!'

'OK.'

'Don't be so smug! They won't come! Leave it!' He almost pleaded, 'Look, just pay him the money and—'

Feiffer paused at the entrance. He said softly to O'Yee, 'All going well, I'll see you a little later.' He went through the en-trance, past the police cars, and began walking at the same easy pace across the graveyard to the ruined church on the hill.

O'Yee hesitated. He glanced over at Spencer and Auden. He looked down the street. No one was coming. He knew they wouldn't. Not the Chinese.

Not them.

O'Yee was in charge. He looked around anxiously.

Mendoza said, smiling, 'How nice, they've let you come for a chat.' He glanced at the dog by his side in the dank little church – all the windows were smashed and he had a clear view of the rows of Chinese tombs and headstones from one and the police and their cars from the other – and said patronizingly, 'Mr Feiffer, isn't it? We have met, but you probably don't re-call—' He left the sentence unfinished and smiled again.

It was a very small church, smaller inside than it seemed to be from outside. There were a few rows of broken and rotting pews left in place and a stone lump where the altar had been, even a small oak harmonium to one side covered in dust and masonry chippings. There was a little curtain separating the entrance to the bell tower. It was red, a thick material gone frayed and rotten with age. Small animals had been in the church: there were dried droppings on the flagstone floor. Mendoza said urbanely, 'Mr Feiffer ... ?'

Feiffer looked at him. He saw the walkie-talkie style transmitter in Mendoza's hand. In his other hand there was something else. It was the battery-powered toothbrush. Mendoza said, 'If you've quite finished your little inspection, I'd like to have a little chat about the method of delivering the money.' He said pleasantly, 'If you don't find it too inconvenient.'

Feiffer nodded. He went to one of the windows – the one facing the street – and looked out.

'It's all for show.' He patted the dog, became bored, and sat at the end of one of the pews. He said, 'The rifles aren't loaded.' The dog came up and sat down docilely on the flagstones beside him. Mendoza said, 'No need to feel so thwarted, Harry.' He asked, 'I may call you Harry, may I?'

Feiffer looked at him. He didn't like what he saw. 'Where's the gun?'

'What gun?'

'Your gun. The Mauser.' He said, 'One 7·63mm Mauser broomhandle automatic pistol, serial number 551296. Where is it?'

Mendoza said, 'You've checked the Arms Licence!'

'I checked the Arms Licence. Where's the weapon?'

Mendoza smiled. He nodded to the dog and then patted him on the head. He thought he had been right to pick Feiffer as the one to deal with on the lower level. He was thorough. If you wanted something from someone, thoroughness was another way of saying slavish predictability. He had been, as usual, utterly right. Mendoza said, 'At the quarry, of course. It's not supposed to be removed from the premises.' He said, 'Would I do anything illegal? It's still at the quarry.' He glanced surreptitiously out of the window at the police cars and repeated, 'It's not here.' He asked, 'Did you expect it would be?'

'I'm in two minds about it.'

'Send someone to the quarry to check.'

'The security safe where the gun is kept is locked. You've got the keys.'

'So I do!' Mendoza said, 'I threw them away.' He glanced again at the cars and police a distance away at the cemetery entrance and said quickly, 'I haven't got the gun. OK?'

'No, it isn't OK.'

'Well what do you expect me to do about it?'

Feiffer said, 'I expect you to give me the keys so I can send someone around to verify that the weapon is where it's supposed to be.'

'I threw the keys away!'

'Did you?'

'Yes!' The dog got up and moved forward restively. Mendoza restrained him, 'I threw them away.' He said, 'I haven't got a gun. All right?'

Feiffer said evenly, 'I take it that the transmitter in your hand is the detonating device?'

Mendoza nodded. He smiled.

'And the other thing – just what purpose does that serve?' It was the battery toothbrush. It seemed to have been amended in some way – Feiffer was no expert on electric toothbrushes, but somehow it didn't look right – it was screwed on to a length of wood with two clamps on it. Feiffer said, 'Well?'

Mendoza smiled at him. Mendoza said, 'You'll probably never know.'

'What does that mean?' Feiffer walked unhurriedly towards the harmonium and ran his hand along it. It was thick with dust and there was rot in it. A section of the veneer came off in his hand. 'Well? What does that mean?'

'You can't jump me, Harry. Not before I press the button.'

Feiffer said, 'I see.' He walked towards the curtained bell tower and stopped. He glanced back at Mendoza's face. Mendoza had stood up to keep him in view, but there was no alarm on his face. Feiffer said, 'Why political?'

'I was wondering when you were going to get to that.'

'Oh, I know why you did it. I was just hoping to hear your rationalization—' He stopped. 'What "rationalization" means is—'

'I know what it means! Don't you think I'm stupid!' He put a hand on the dog's neck to keep him under control. 'Don't you start trying to be clever with me! I'm a European, not one of your stupid little Chinks!' He ordered Feiffer, 'Just you remember that!'

Feiffer said, 'If the Chinese knew what you were up to here, bombs or no bombs, they'd tear you to ribbons—'

'But they're not going to know, are they?'

'Hence "political".'

'Hence "political".' Mendoza said, 'It's a matter between European gentlemen.' He said suddenly candidly, 'I'm not even so certain the Chinks would care about the graves anyway. Europeans might think they would, but I'm not so sure they would at all.'

'So I've been told just a few minutes ago by someone else.'

Mendoza said, 'They're stupid, you see. The Chinks.' Feiffer moved towards the altar and touched the surface of the stone stump. Mendoza said, 'Stop walking!' (Feiffer stopped and turned to look at him.) Mendoza moved a little into the light of one of the empty windows. In his civilian clothes, he looked like a tall, well-dressed, smooth-faced lizard. He had no lines on his face at all. He said, 'Do you want me to tell you about the Chinks, Harry? I'd be delighted.' He said, 'I know all about them and their superstitions—'

'From your friend Mr Tam?'

'That leper!' Mendoza said, 'Come over here! Stand by the window!' He said, 'I'll tell you all about them.' His voice changed. It dropped, became intimate. He said, 'Listen, Harry, you don't have to pretend you think they're as good as us with me.' He said, 'I'm a fellow European, I know the truth.' He said coaxingly, 'You don't have to pretend with me.'

Feiffer glanced up at the roof. It was crossbeamed with old, black timber gone rotten. He glanced at his watch.

Mendoza said, 'Listen!'

Feiffer gazed at him. He knew the gun was there somewhere. He kept trying to find the place it might be hidden.

O'Yee glanced down the street. It was cordoned off at both ends. He thought, 'They won't come.' He looked over at Auden and Spencer and the ineffectual rifles. He thought, 'It's Feiffer thinking he knows all about the Chinese. About graves and burials and the importance of superstition.' He thought, 'But he's wrong. It's all right for Conway Kan to say I was right about the bodies in the water, but the ordinary people don't care.' He thought, 'They were just there for the morbid pleasure of it.' He thought, 'No one really believes in those things any more.' He thought, 'Oh they all buy lottery tickets and talk about luck and good numbers, but when it comes to the big things they just don't care.' He thought, 'They won't come.'

He thought, 'If they do and there's a riot, it'll be the end of Feiffer.'

He thought, 'No one'll come.'

He thought, 'No.' He glanced back down the street.

Apart from the police, it was deserted.

Mendoza put the battery toothbrush in the pocket of his shirt. He looked hopefully at Feiffer. Feiffer couldn't think what purpose it could possibly serve. Mendoza said, 'No?' He patted the pocket and glanced down at the tone-send button on the transmitter in his hand. 'Where's Conway Kan now?'

Feiffer said, 'He's getting the money.'

'Hmm.' Mendoza said donnishly, 'What you don't seem to understand, Harry – or what you make out for the sake of appearances that you don't understand, is that the Chinese are garbage.' He nodded to himself in absolute seriousness. 'People like the Chinese are only there to be made use of.' He said, 'As a European you appreciate that.' He said, 'Of course, you do. That's why the European police here take bribes—' He added, 'I happen to know it doesn't happen at your station for some reason, but it happens everywhere else. The reason it happens is that Europeans, once they get here, realize that as far as civilized societies are concerned, anything that happens in Hong Kong or Macao or places like that – where there are Chinks – just isn't on the same wavelength. It just doesn't matter. It's a sign of strength, understanding the niggers – it just doesn't matter—'

'Oh, yes?'

'Yes.'

'It's not because the people who are as corrupt as hell are usually people who have always been corrupt as hell anywhere? He said, 'I can think of one or two notable examples off hand.' He said more for his own benefit, 'If you consider the Welsh to be Europeans.' He glanced at Mendoza, saw he didn't know what he meant and that he didn't like not knowing, and said, 'Go on with your theory.'

Mendoza said, 'I'm going to blow up their cemetery and there's nothing you can do about it!'

'I don't suppose there is.' Mendoza hadn't liked not knowing. Feiffer said ingratiatingly, 'I just wanted to meet you. You out-manoeuvred me all down the line and I wanted to meet you before you left.' He said, 'I assume you are leaving the Colony?'

'No.'

'Oh?'

Mendoza said, 'Why should I?' He said, 'I understand them: the Chinks. I'm staying. I'm going to buy a house on the Peak and live in full view.'

'Are you serious?'

Mendoza said, 'They like being tricked, the Chinks. They spend their lives trying to trick people and trying to lord it over them—' He said, 'The way they do at the quarry. Thirty years ago I would have been in charge of that place! But I have to say this for them: once they know you know you're better than they are, that you're cleverer, that you've out-tricked them better than they ever could have done, then they respect you.' He said to Feiffer, 'I'll be all right. I'll live in luxury and respect for the rest of my life.' He said quietly, 'You have to admit the whole thing's absolutely brilliant – the immunity and everything.' He said, 'It's really absolutely brilliant.' He said realistically, 'I suppose I'll have to have a few personal bodyguards, but then everyone does.'

Feiffer paused. He said, 'Let me understand this – you intend to extort almost a million American dollars from someone on the threat that you destroy this cemetery. Right?'

Mendoza said happily, 'Yes.'

'On the assumption that, in reality, he, like the rest of the Chinese, really don't give a stuff about it—'

'Good, yes! Good!'

'And because he doesn't give a stuff about it, he isn't going to tell anyone that he paid the money and you'll be able to live on here safely? Is that the theory?'

Mendoza nodded. Really, a man like Feiffer would be an ideal – Mendoza said, 'Yes, yes!'

'Hence *political*, to enable Conway Kan to keep it quiet.'

'Correct.'

Feiffer paused. He said, 'You're right, it is bloody brilliant.' He asked, 'But why should Conway Kan bother to pay the money if what you say about the Chinese is true? Why not just let you blow it to hell?'

Mendoza said, 'Because he wants to keep in with the Euro-

peans who do believe that the Chinese care about superstition!'
He said, 'Do you see? It's perfect!'

Feiffer said quietly, 'Why not just hold a person to ransom?' He said evenly, 'This all seems a bit complicated when you could have achieved the same ends – even immunity – by something a lot simpler?' He said piercingly, 'Or is there one little variable in the equation that you'd rather have left out?' He said, 'Something that has some sort of bearing on that thing in your shirt pocket.' He said, 'And on the gun you claim you don't have?' He put it to Mendoza, 'If you're so bloody brilliant, why didn't you leave the keys to the security safe at the quarry so we could make sure the gun was there?'

Mendoza said irritably, 'What's the gun got to do with it? Forget about the gun! It's the rest of it – it's genius! Isn't it? I really used them, didn't I? The Chinks! I've really ground them into the dirt!'

Feiffer sniffed. He kept wondering about the electric toothbrush. It seemed totally incongruous, out of place. He glanced at Mendoza's hand around the walkie-talkie. The knuckles gripping it were white with strain. Feiffer said, 'What are you frightened of?'

'I'm not afraid of anything!'

'Then why have you got the gun hidden here somewhere? And why won't you tell me the purpose of that thing in your pocket?' Feiffer said, 'And why go for a complicated plan when you could have achieved the same ends by a simple one?' He asked, 'Is it because if you threatened the life of a human being the police would have the right to shoot you?'

Mendoza's face knotted. There was a tiny nerve under his eye. He swallowed.

Feiffer said, 'People who kill by stealth are always cowards.' He said quietly, 'That's been my experience.' He asked Mendoza softly, 'So what are you frightened of?'


O'Yee rubbed his cheek with his hand. He looked along the road. He thought they wouldn't come. He thought, 'I don't know. I'm not sure.' He thought, 'Why do it? It's crazy!' He thought, 'He must have been insane getting Ho to organize a riot.' He thought, 'Even a crowd!' He thought, 'They won't come!' He thought, 'Fucking Chinese! They don't even care!'

He thought, 'Maybe they'll come.' He thought, 'I don't know!' He went to the Emergency Unit van and ordered the ammunition issued for the Armalite rifles. He glanced at the Chinese Constables. They did nothing.

He thought, 'They won't come.' He looked across at the church. It was silent and dark. God only knew what was happening in there. He thought, 'Well that's appropriate anyway.'

Auden and Spencer had full magazines of cartridges in their hands. They hesitated before snapping them into the Armalites. Spencer put his on the ground.

O'Yee thought, 'I've got to do something.' He glanced at the Chinese Constables. He had no idea what they were thinking. One of them undid the flap button on his holster and ran his hand over the butt of his Police Positive. O'Yee thought, 'Maybe they're on my side.' He glanced at Yan. Yan nodded. He had been the one with the flap.

O'Yee threw a quick look in the direction of the church. He thought suddenly, 'I've got to do something—'

He shouted out in a stentorian voice, '*Load your weapons!*'

Mendoza screamed at Feiffer, 'What are they doing?' There was a terrible fear in his eyes. His hand shook on the plastic body of the walkie-talkie. He touched at the toothbrush in his pocket. He shouted at Feiffer, 'I'm not threatening anybody!'

Feiffer said quickly, 'They're getting ready.' He thought, 'O'Yee's jumped the gun!' He tried to make the right move. He said clearly and loudly, 'I've laid on a riot. I've had the word passed that you're going to destroy this place and there are three thousand people coming with the sole intention of tearing your heart out. The police are getting ready to protect you if you give yourself up.' He said, 'You've got about fifteen minutes to decide. After that you'll be on your own and there'll be no one. The police are going to leave.' He said to Mendoza, 'If you're so afraid of dying then you're in big trouble.' He said, 'It isn't going to be done quietly between gentlemen – people are going to come here and kill you.'

'Nonsense!'

Feiffer said, 'They're coming. I spoke to someone on the radio before I came here and they're coming. You've got about fifteen minutes to make up your mind to surrender.'

Mendoza paused. Feiffer could hear his breath coming in

short spasms. The dog looked from one of them to the other in confusion. He didn't know what to do either. Mendoza said, 'They won't come!'

'They're coming now!'

'Then you have to protect me! The police have to protect me!' He shouted at Feiffer, 'I've thought of everything! You have to protect me!'

'No.'

'The police can't let people be murdered. Not even criminals. They have to protect criminals from their victims.' He moved quickly away from the window and grabbed the dog by the collar to pull him next to him for protection, 'It's your *duty* to protect me!'

Feiffer drew a breath. He thought, 'Well, here it comes—' He said quietly, 'We can't.'

Mendoza said, 'Ha!'

'We can't because you've got immunity. Or you will have. You're immune from prosecution.'

'So what?'

' "So what" is that *we're* not. If we helped you against a crowd of honest, law-abiding citizens, we'd be acting as accomplices to your crime. Extortion. We'd be assisting you.' He said quietly, 'Since you can't be arrested, there's no way we could justify our behaviour by saying that we were acting in the expectation of an arrest because, well, you can't be arrested.' He said, 'What we'd be doing, according to any sort of logic or legal argument, is assisting in the execution of a crime – and of course, we can't do that.' He said to Mendoza in a reasonable voice, 'All I can suggest to you is that you'd be well-advised to give up the idea of immunity completely before the crowd of honest, law-abiding, murderous Chinese gets here.' He asked, 'Don't you agree?' He said pleasantly, 'I'll take the transmitter if you want somewhere to put it . . .'

Mendoza looked at him.

Feiffer said, 'I estimate, fifteen minutes '

Mendoza stared at him.

Feiffer smiled encouragingly, 'Or less—' He waited.

It was irresistible. It might blow it, but it was irresistible. Feiffer said very softly, 'It's bloody brilliant, you have to admit . . .'

*

O'Yee moved forward towards the entrance to the cemetery. He thought bitterly, 'It's all just a goddamned mockery. No one's coming because no one cares.' He thought, 'They don't care: the Chinese. The Europeans are the only ones who think this sort of thing is important to the Chinese. The Chinese don't. It's just a mockery.' He thought with hatred, 'Or half-caste mongrels like me. People like me who don't know what side of the fence they're supposed to perch on.' He thought, 'People like me who don't know whether they should have been white, yellow, or pink with green spots.' He thought, 'The crowd won't come.' He thought, 'They wouldn't come on the beach. If I'd called to them on the beach they wouldn't have come. I'm running around in circles trying to suck up to a real Chinese – find his fucking toucan – because all I really want is for someone to say to me, "They care. You're a real Chinese and you were right, they really do care about things like that".' He thought, 'And it's all balls! If I really was a Chinese then I wouldn't care and that's what being Chinese means.' He thought, almost in tears, 'Lousy Chinks. It'll be the end of Feiffer for suggesting it and they won't come. They never do anything for anyone.' He stood at the cemetery entrance and found he had his hand around the butt of his holstered gun. He thought, '*I* BLOODYWELL CARE!'

He began running for the church, consumed with hatred.

Mendoza said, 'No!!' He shrieked at Feiffer, 'They won't come!' He screamed, 'You've got it wrong and they won't come! I *know*!!'

'You bloodywell don't know! You think they will come otherwise you wouldn't have gone to such trouble to make sure no one knew! You know they'll come and you know exactly what they'll do to you! You don't hate them – you're afraid of them! That's the wellspring of your sort of superiority – bloody, unbridled *fear*! And they'll kill you stone bloody dead, make no mistake about it!'

'Then I'll blow the whole lot of them straight to hell!'

'Balls!' He glanced at the dog. It had started snarling.

'I'll blow them to hell.'

Feiffer stopped. He said, 'You've got fifteen minutes.' He glanced anxiously at the dog. 'I'll wait outside for exactly fifteen minutes and then, when the crowd comes, I intend to order my men back to their Stations.' He heard a noise behind him, near the front door to the church, in the little stone covered vestibule. He thought it must be a rat or a mouse. He said, 'Fifteen minutes.' His eyes rested on the shirt pocket where the toothbrush was. 'Fifteen minutes.'

Mendoza shook his head.

'Fifteen minutes.' He started for the door.

Mendoza said, 'No.' It was dark by the door. Something stirred behind one of the pews there. Mendoza said, 'You're bluffing.'

'Am I?' There was another sound, different, a long way off. It sounded like a moaning sound, or an engine – a heavy engine working deep underwater or in a tunnel.

Mendoza said, 'Yes.'

Feiffer knew what it was. 'I'll wait outside.' He went to the main door and stepped out into the vestibule. The dog came after him with his eyes glittering. He was making sure Feiffer went outside. The noise was there again. The dog sensed it. His ears pricked up. He became uneasy. The dog knew what the sound was too. He could smell something cold and ominous in the air, like the precursor to a storm. Mendoza shouted to the dog, 'Guard!!' He slammed the door behind Feiffer and left him standing in the vestibule with the dog.

The dog sniffed. There was something coming. The noise was growing louder.

Inside the church, Mendoza went to the window to see what the sound was. He looked across the graveyard towards the entrance of the cemetery. He had his back to the interior of the church. There was a slight rustle behind him. He heard the sound from the street getting louder and louder. In the vestibule, Feiffer glanced at the dog. He put his hand in his pocket for a cigarette to appear calm. The dog looked enormous.

It was the crowd. There were two thousand of them. Mendoza stared out of the window. There was another rustle behind him. He couldn't believe it: they came as a dark moving mass, like a tide. They flowed down the street and the cordons seemed to disappear under them. The police weren't doing anything! He touched at the radio transmitter. It seemed to have lost all its potence. He thought of Feiffer. He turned and faced the closed door. He knew Feiffer was out there with the dog. He looked back to the crowd. He had the electric toothbrush. It was his ace in the hole. He reached in and touched it. He thought, 'Feiffer—'

He touched at the toothbrush and knew what to do with it. He—

O'Yee shouted at him, 'YOU LOUSY MOTHERFUCKER!' and leapt at him. He took the first blow on his arm. The transmitter went spinning out of his hand. It was a Chink! Mendoza fought back like a madman. He shrieked out to the dog in the vestibule with Feiffer, *Kill him!*

The people in the crowd were shouting.

Auden stood up with the Armalite. He heard the crowd. He turned and saw them streaming down the road like lunatics. Spencer saw them. He saw someone in the crowd he knew. It was Frances. He thought, 'Oh, no ...' He said to Auden, 'Don't shoot!' There was a terrible snarling sound. He saw the dog at Feiffer's throat outside the church. He raised his rifle. The dog and the man fell over on to the ground and were rolling around near one of the headstones. He saw Frances coming towards him. He looked at the Chinese Constables. They were moving towards the crowd waving their arms. Someone came to the hole in the wall near the tower. It was Mendoza. Then there was someone hanging on to him and pulling him back. Then he was gone. Something came flying out, thrown. It was a little box. The transmitter. He saw O'Yee at the hole go out after the box. He made it to the ground and grabbed it. There was a flurry of movement from inside the church. O'Yee was on his feet running towards Feiffer and the dog.

In the church, Mendoza ran to the bell tower. The Mauser was laid out on a flagstone, fully loaded, with stripper clips of ammunition in rows beside it. He snapped the battery toothbrush on to the side of the gun and slipped a wire loop at the end of the brush lever around the trigger. He drew back the hammer, aimed it at O'Yee though an empty window and pressed the battery button on the body of the toothbrush.

The Mauser held ten rounds. It threw them all out in one explosive half second burst.

Spencer saw O'Yee go down. Auden started firing at the tower.

*

The ground subsided around him. He hadn't been hit. He couldn't believe it. O'Yee grabbed the transmitter and rolled back against the stone wall of the church. He tried to get the transmitter apart. The aerial was short and too strong. There was a screw in the battery compartment. It was tight. He ripped at it with his fingernails. Nothing. He drew his revolver and fired a shot at the bell tower. Mendoza had another clip of ten rounds in the magazine. He touched the electric button. The ten rounds ripped out over O'Yee's head. O'Yee snapped open the cylinder of his gun and got the fired case out. He tried the lip of the brass against the screw notch. It was the right width. He started wrenching at the empty case to turn one sharp side of it into a screw-driver. The case was still hot. He dropped it.

The crowd were on their faces in the street. A burst of ten shots flew out from the bell tower and tore wedges from the stone fence to the street. Auden got a quick bead on the bell tower window and loosed off a magazine on full automatic. The bell tower disappeared into a flurry of dust stems. He tore at another magazine and rammed it into the Armalite. He looked at Spencer.

Spencer was on his feet, running. He went towards Frances. There was another flurry of shots. They passed over his head. Auden took aim and banged three rounds into the tower. Auden looked over at Feiffer. He couldn't see anything.

Feiffer had his hands around the dog's throat. It was incredibly strong. He tried to hold it off. There seemed to be teeth and claws everywhere. He felt one of the claws rip through his coat and catch him down the arm. He squeezed with every ounce of strength at the dog's larynx. The dog stopped snarling. Its eyes bulged. He thought he had it. Then it pulled away and he felt its breath on his face. It was going for his throat. Feiffer hung on and squeezed. He tried to get to his feet. He slipped over. He heard a burst of gunfire. He scrabbled to one knee with his hands still around the dog's throat, holding him off. He got half upright and tried to scrabble the dog towards the wall of the church. The dog gyrated and fought back. It had muscles like steel. He got to the church wall out of the line of fire and tried to twist the dog against the wall. The dog got its teeth into his arm and ground them in. He got the dog to the wall and twisted it away. He wanted to bash its head against the wall. It was too strong.

It fought back. He was losing. His strength was going. Feiffer knew he was losing.

Spencer said, 'Frances!' He raced across the street to where Frank lay on the ground. She seemed to be crying.

Auden loosed off another three rounds. He couldn't see him. He shouted at the tower, 'Where are you, you bastard?' He shouted at the tower, 'Bastard!' He saw Feiffer momentarily. The dog had him. Auden shouted to Spencer, 'Cover!' He knew Feiffer would be dead by the time it was over. He shouted to Spencer, 'Cover me, you lousy fox-hunting man!' and Spencer turned and had the Armalite in his hands, crouching next to Frances in the street. Spencer shouted, 'She's not hit!' as Auden went over the wall towards the church.

O'Yee got the screw loose. The batteries were inside. He tore them out. He pressed the tone-send button. Nothing. He shouted at someone, 'It's safe!' as Mendoza sent a wild burst at where Auden was running across the graveyard.

Auden made it to the dog. He tried to get a shot in. There seemed to be blood everywhere. The dog's head came out of the flurry and he bayoneted it through the ear with the gun barrel. He actually felt the muzzle penetrate bone and brain. He pulled the trigger. There was a terrible thump and a frenzy of movement and the thing was dead. He looked up at the bell tower. He saw Mendoza for a moment. Mendoza had the Mauser trained on the crowd. He ripped something from the side of the gun and took a single aimed shot. Auden tried to move back to get in a shot but the angle was too great.

At the crowd, standing over Frank, Spencer saw Mendoza's face between the cross-hairs of the telescopic sight. He could almost feel Frank's life next to his feet. He squeezed the trigger with a feeling of ice in his heart.

It was a single shot among many, but it echoed, and went on echoing around the cemetery for what seemed a very long time.

Auden was helping Feiffer to his feet. There was something hanging half-way out of the window of the bell tower. It looked like a dark clothed lizard.

Auden looked back at Spencer. He was standing very still, like a statue, with the gun still trained on the window. Someone was standing next to him, a girl. Auden waited. Spencer did not shoot again.

*

**6 p.m.**

The Commander waited until Doctor Macarthur's people had taken the covered stretcher out through the main entrance of the cemetery. He looked at Feiffer, O'Yee, Auden and Spencer. They seemed to be waiting for him to say something. Feiffer had his arm bandaged and one sleeve of his coat gone.

The Commander said, 'Well ...' He looked at the crowd. They were standing about in knots waiting for the uniformed men with magnetometers to locate the last of the bombs. He said to Feiffer, 'I suppose you expect me to say that laying on a riot was a bad idea.' He glanced over at Ho talking to a few people by one of the tombs and sighed. He said quietly, 'Quite frankly, I'm not that much of an old dog. I'm not that up on the behaviour of Chinese crowds.' He said quietly, 'I'm glad someone around here is.'

Feiffer winced with the pain from the anti-tetanus shot. 'I didn't really expect they'd come.' He said, 'It was a bluff.'

O'Yee said, 'I precipitated it. I overreacted.'

The commander said, 'Hmm.' He gave the impression he was reasonably happy about that too.

O'Yee said, 'I'm sorry.'

The Commander opened his hands dismissively to wave that aside. He said to O'Yee, 'You're the Chinese, not me.' He said humbly to Auden, 'We all live and learn, Phil, don't we?'

Auden looked at him. He didn't quite know what to say. He thought he meant about Special Branch. Auden was happy where he was. Auden said, 'If you say so, sir.'

The Commander nodded. He looked tired. He walked back to his car thinking about Korea.

Feiffer had told Ho to tell the crowd the cemetery was being reopened for new business. The one with the best feng shui in Hong Kong. The crowd had known nothing about Mendoza. He hadn't been sure that if they had known, they would have come. He looked at O'Yee.

Political.

Best to say nothing. Still, maybe they—

O'Yee smiled happily at him.

Feiffer said nothing.

**9 p.m.**

She was gone. Feiffer went through the apartment looking for a message, but there was none there. He thought she had probably just stepped out for a moment to talk to someone in one of the other apartments or to watch television with them. He went to the bed and lay on it fully dressed and thought about Mendoza. There was a horrible looking thing, half wrapped in a brown paper parcel, at the end of the bed. He gave it a kick and it fell on to the floor and rolled out into the living room. Fortunately, it was in a cage. And dead. It was something she had obviously bought to keep her company: it looked like a stuffed toucan. Feiffer thought she had probably picked it up for next to nothing in one of the Thieves' Markets.

He wondered where she was. He took the telephone off the hook before the hospital rang to say that, two hours earlier, his wife had suddenly gone into premature labour, that she was well and that he had a son, and closed his eyes to sleep.

He remembered that O'Yee had promised to come by about midnight for a drink and got up again and put the front door on the latch. The bird, upside down, glared at him with its beady black eyes. He thought the sight of that would blow anyone's evening. He went back to bed and fell asleep wondering where the hell the so-called thieves in the so-called Thieves' Market got something like that in the first place anyway.

O'Yee wrenched open Feiffer's front door with an enormous box of cigars in his hand. He felt marvellous, joyous, the bearer of good tidings. There was a horrible looking thing staring at him upside down on the floor of the apartment and he snapped on the light for a moment to see what it was . . .

William Marshall
## Yellowthread Street

Chief Inspector Feiffer had his hands full . . . tourist troubles, a US
sailor turned stick-up artist, and the jealous Chinese who solved
his marital difficulties with an axe. Then a Mongolian with a kukri
brought an extra touch of terror to the district . . .

'Fast and bloody' YORKSHIRE POST

## The Hatchet Man

A killer on the rampage – shooting his victims while they watch
the screen in the local cinema. The job of hunting him down falls
to Chief Inspector Feiffer and his tough English and Chinese fuzz.
They only get a break when a cop gets a bullet and crazy old
Mrs Mortimer steps in front of a train . . .

Bob Ottum
## The Tuesday Blade

When Glory-Ann came to New York City in search of the
swinging singles scene, the pimps marked her down as a natural.
She had the kind of body that men wanted badly, and that made
her a highly saleable commodity. But Glory-Ann had a razor in her
lovely hand – and she was through with being anybody's victim . . .

Ed McBain
## Blood Relatives

Saturday night, and party night on the Precinct – the perfect
backdrop for a knife-carrying sex attacker. Seventeen year-old
Muriel was stabbed to death and her cousin Patricia got away with
a slashed cheek. When she ran into the station house Kling
watched the bloody hand-prints appear on the glass panel. A
messy start to a case that got messier – every time Patricia changed
her story . . .

## Desmond Lowden
## **Bellman and True**

Hiller used to have a job in computers and a wife. Now he's just
got a step-son and a drinking problem. Coming up behind are the
boys from the East End. They want Hiller because he's got the
computer know-how that makes bank jobs easy . . . And he's open
to persuasion – from boots and knives and fists.

## Clark Howard
## **Mark the Sparrow**

In the state of California you don't have to kill anybody to get a
death sentence. You can go to Death Row on technicalities – like
kidnapping, assault and sexual perversion. That's how they nailed
Weldon Whitman. The State says he's guilty, but Whitman insists
he's innocent. Together, the reporter Robert Cloud and Genevieve
Neller, the law librarian, organize a Save Whitman campaign that
snowballs into a coast-to-coast crusade – but maybe Whitman
isn't innocent after all?

## R. Lance Hill
## **Nails**

Joe Black was a loner – who'd fought to survive every place from
the schoolyard to Fort Worth jail. You can't buy freedom on a
monthly pay cheque and Joe wants the freedom that the big
money can buy . . . So when the rich guy with the clean hands full
of dirty money wants a killing done, Joe's got himself a job . . .